BLACKPOOL CENTRAL
TEL. 23977.

D0552031

30. JUL. 1990

A-2 GEAC

AUTHOR

MORRIS, R.

CLASS
BPFR

TITLE

Vigil

Vigil

Vigil

Roberta Morris

Williams-Wallace Publishers Inc.

Published in 1986 by
Williams-Wallace Publishers Inc.
2 Silver Avenue
Toronto, Canada
M6R 3A2

ISBN 0-88795-052-3 (bound)
ISBN 0-88795-049-3 (pbk.)

Canadian Cataloguing in Publication Data

Morris, Roberta, 1953 -
  Vigil   041135861

ISBN 0-88795-052-3 (bound) - ISBN 0-88795-049-3 (pbk.)

I. Title.

PS8576.077V53 1986   C813'.54   C86-093433-0
PR9199.3.M64V53 1986

Cover art: Debbie Ledwon

Author photo: Merle Addison

Published with the generous assistance of the Canada Council and the Ontario Arts Council.

Printed and bound in Canada.

Acknowledgements

Special thanks to my husband, David Giuffrida, and to Polly Thompson, John Trainor, Vera Szöke, Paul Lang, Liz Hart and Ann Wallace for all their support and assistance. I am also grateful to Fran Morris and Irish Kikuchi for their assistance with research, and to Pat Jeffries, the Physicians for Social Responsibility, the SCM students, and the many peace activists who challenged me to think more deeply about the threat of nuclear war.

For Andréa, Nathaniel and Mary

1

It was Jan Ito's turn.

"Brand-new maternity pants. Pants that fit," she said, hoisting up the baggy pants she was wearing. A rope threaded through the belt loops held them over her pregnant abdomen.

Camille pushed her damp, strangly hair away from her face and took her turn. "Those little smile buttons people wore. Do you remember those little faces? The smile buttons."

"Morphine," Bea said. She squatted at the edge of the taro paddy, scratching words in her notebook, hardly looking up to take her turn. Her black bag was open beside her. The cuff she had just used for taking Jan's blood-pressure hung out the top of the bag, its velcro edge dangling in the mud.

Jan and Camille were digging in the upper paddy, dividing taro roots for transplanting into the lower paddy. Below them, five other women had been working hard all morning, preparing the lower paddy to be flooded.

"I've got it," Jan smiled. "Shrink-wrapped cucumbers. All clean and ready to slice. Chilled cucumber slices."

"Popsicles," Camille said.

"Stouffer's Lean Cuisine Corn Souffle," Bea said, without looking up.

Jan wrinkled her nose. "Long-distance phone calls."

"Dream Whip," Camille said, pulling out a large root and shaking off the dirt that clung underneath the tuber.

"My fountain pen."

"Frozen pizza."

"Creamsicles."

"Sterile gauze."

Jan laughed. "Come on, Dr. Bea. You miss sterile gauze?"

"Yes, I do."

"I don't believe it."

Bea clapped her notebook shut. "What is this, Jan? Making up new rules? It isn't enough that I play this silly game; now I must convince you that I do, in fact, miss these things?" Bea sighed. "Well, I pass."

"Fine. Sara Lee Frozen Pound Cake. Your turn, Camille," Jan said, slinging a shovelful of wet dirt onto the bank.

"Macadamia nut ice cream. Eating macadamia nut ice cream in front of the T.V. Oh, and watching Johnny Carson. Gosh, I miss Johnny," Camille said.

Bea pushed her glasses up on the bridge of her nose and looked over at Camille. "Now look who's breaking the rules. That's two things you named there, dear. Ice cream and Johnny Carson. If you get two things in one turn, I do too: sterile gauze and cigarettes."

"It's your turn, Jan," Camille said.

"My roto-tiller."

"Frozen bananas dipped in chocolate with peanuts on them."

"Ultrasound."

Jan dug her shovel into the ground, and jumped onto the edge of it to plunge it deeper. The spade tip chipped on a buried rock. "Shit. My shovel tip broke," she mumbled.

The game was over for the moment.

While the women worked, their children played on the edge of the paddies, dipping their toy shovels into the water. These work days were the children's favorite days. Now, three months after the women had begun work, five months since they'd come back outdoors late in April, the taro plants were several inches high.

We can't let up now, Jan thought, looking at the fragile green stalks. Without enough food we'll get weak; our imaginations will run wild. The kids have been sucking on sugar cane a lot, but that won't hold them forever. Got to get food or their imaginations will run wild.

Since last April, Jan had kept her own imagination in careful check. Last April was when they'd been cut off. Without notice, the electricity was off all across the island. Lights went out. Radios and T.V.s went dead. Jan had switched on the transistor radio but she couldn't get a signal. She'd tried the phone but the lines were dead. It was the same in all the small villages and towns across Kaane, and gradually the knowledge that they had accommodated since childhood came into focus: they were targeted. There were a few moments of panic, neighbors running first from room to room, then door to door. But it was just a matter of moments before the panic subsided. Everyone braced themselves. A calm settled over the towns and villages. They waited.

During the two weeks that followed, some young soldiers—there were maybe twenty soldiers stationed on the island—ordered everyone to take shelter and stay in their homes. These men were on Kaane to staff the satellite tracking station perched up on top of Halepele. For a while they were obeyed. People huddled indoors and heard nothing from the outside other than the soldiers' bullhorns bellowing. Then there were three days of complete silence, and then, on the third day, the satellite tracking station up on Halepele exploded. Then again, the silence. It had already begun raining, and nothing was heard above the pelting of the rain and wind against window glass. It rained heavily for eight days, before tapering off into a slow drizzle that lasted another two weeks.

Now, most people believed it was the rain that killed.

Standing at the edge of the upper paddy, Jan turned her head to look across the mountain. Below her the green canefields cut into the brown ranchlands near Ahupuaa. Above her the dark green groves of kukui, banyan, even some tall pines, blanketed the higher levels of the mountain. Toward the top of Halepele there was a crater left behind by the explosion, and it stared down on the island like a blind eye. As Jan looked up at the crater, she recalled the blast; it was the only sound she had heard from outside during those first two weeks in April when she and Michael huddled, with their two sons between them, in the dug-out part of their split-level. During those two weeks that had seemed to stretch out into oblivion, the blast was the only thing that gave substance to the sensation: something has happened. Jan's family lived in Lono, far enough up on the mountain so that the explosion had shaken their house.

"Holy Christ," Jan had groaned and grabbed her two sons. "This is it." And then the uninterrupted silence engulfed them again.

Before everyone recognized that the blast wasn't a missile, the blast had kindled the hope that there were survivors off the island, even if their only interest in Kaane was to bomb it. But apparently it was dynamite that leveled the station, and Michael had speculated that the blast was an inside job, the army cleaning up after itself so that the espionage carried out at the tracking station wouldn't be discovered. His theory had seemed more credible than most to Jan, until it was learned that the sergeant had died in the explosion; it didn't seem likely to her that he would have blown himself up.

Jan had not wasted time speculating on what she couldn't know. Since April, she had raised practicality to the level of a religion, and there was no room for extraneous considerations. Food and her children counted most. Then Michael. What followed in her line-up of practical values was a long list of tradeable goods. The non-tradeable goods—the things that were gone—were just memories the women made lists of while they worked. That is how the game had begun. They remembered. They remembered everything.

The mud was thick in the taro paddy and Jan's feet sank deep into it. As she pulled her long red hair, now streaked with mud, into a knot at the back of her neck, she breathed in the smell of the rich wet soil.

Camille worked quietly now, piling mud onto the mounds and picking out the taro plants that were to be divided and moved into the new paddy. Jan stood, resting her weight on one foot and then the other so the mud squeezed between her toes. For just a moment she was caught up by the heaviness of her pregnant body. She felt the baby move. She felt hungry. Poi, the thick green paste made from the taro root, would be everyone's staple food soon. In time, Jan knew, she would be able to trade poi for fish.

Teruko Masaoka hadn't been playing the game. She was shuffling back and forth on short, thick legs between the upper and lower paddies, loosening the dirt that prevented the water from draining. Now she stooped down into the mud next to Camille and examined the large green leaves that poked up on frail stalks. "It's spindly. It's still not right."

"Maybe that's just the way it grows now," Bea called over to them, while she rummaged around for a pencil in her black doctor's bag. "Jan. Come here for a minute. Did I get your temperature yet? Did I write it down? What did I say your temperature was?"

"It was 98.8, Dr. Bea. Oh, for God's sake, forget it. What do you need it for?"

"Just a routine check-up. Okay." She scratched down the number on the inside flap of her file folder, and without looking up she called out, "Teri, did you get Marilyn's temperature down? How about her blood pressure?" But Teruko didn't hear the question. Bea scribbled one last note into her notebook before stuffing it into her bag, and she got up to leave. She stretched, straightening her skirt, and looked down at the lower paddy where Marilyn Nakatsura was digging. "I have to be going now. Look, Teri, if you didn't get it, I'll just take Marilyn's temperature another day. She certainly does look fine, doesn't she? Just fine."

"I thought you were going to give us a hand here today, Dr. Bea," Jan said.

"Oh yes," Bea nodded. "So I was. Okay. Well, what is it you wanted me to do?"

"This taro has to be transplanted into that mud."

"Okay. Let me just give it a try." Bea lumbered over to pick up a shovel, pushed it into the mud and lifted it, missing the taro root altogether. She slapped the shovelful of mud onto the retaining wall.

Teruko had planned the project well. The location was good, close to Lono where most of the women lived, yet far enough down-country that they could meet traders from the beach and get the fish and seaweed they needed.

Jan glanced over at Bea's curved back. How does Dr. Bea keep the weight on? Jan wondered. Bea still looked bulky. It was only a year ago that Jan had mentioned to another patient, while sitting in Bea's waiting room, that the doctor wasn't as old as she looked. Dr. Bea was only fifty-two, but her grey hair, the dark weathered skin, the extra weight she carried, made her look older. Now Jan envied Bea the pounds. Jan glanced down at her own body and saw her hip bones jutting out on either side of her swollen abdomen. She was nearly five months pregnant; she knew she needed more food. Where was Bea getting food?

11

Jan stretched to breathe and looked down the slope to where the women in the lower paddy stooped into their work. The small paddy reflected the clear sky that met the sea in the distance. She bent down to pick up her broken shovel tip and slipped it into her pocket. As she straightened, she noticed a small spade that someone had dropped which would do nicely for the transplanting. Picking up a bundle of shoots, she began plugging them into the mud while her mind wandered back to her own shovel. Where can I ever get a new one? she asked herself. No one's going to trade a spade for anything now.

Before April no one cared much that things broke down. The government had predicted there would be survivors of an attack, yet they had never noted this particular problem: things break. Jan remembered bits of reports—the parts printed in newspapers—and she recalled one report in particular that had said an all-out exchange would set the economy back to the level it had been in 1920. She had read that one aloud to Michael. Michael had laughed. Weren't those roaring years, the 1920s? After the war we'll be riding Model Ts instead of Hondas, he'd said. But the reports had never said that there wouldn't be any parts available, or that shovels chip.

Bea shook her head and called over to Jan, "If your shovel's broken, then take a break. You've got to take it easier, woman."

Jan glared back and then ignored her.

Camille smiled.

As Jan glanced at Camille's pale face, she realized that Camille's skin was even more pale now than it had been ten years ago when Camille and Ralph had first moved to Kaane. Before moving there, Camille had lived in Texas, San Francisco and Detroit, but for all her moving around, and despite the fact that she was now thirty-five, she still had the appearance and the gangly frame of a teenager. Her hair had bleached almost white and now hung around her face in strands like wet feathers. With her pale pink skin, barely covered by a thin, wet, cotton dress, Camille reminded Jan of an absurd flamingo. Jan watched as Camille slowly picked her way through the wet dirt, wandering down to join the other women in the lower paddy.

Even since April, Camille's face had remained calm. Tension only showed when she chewed on her cuticles or started humming old hymns, as she often did when she was waiting for the game to start. If it didn't start, Camille would continue humming while she worked, sometimes looking over at the others, hoping someone might sing along with her. No one ever did. Before April, Camille's religion sometimes had made her friends feel awkward; now her boundless enthusiasm for it completely unnerved them.

Further below on the mountain, almost at the foot of the mountain, Jan saw the wind blowing against the sugar cane, producing variations of color like green waves meeting the white waves that lapped up on the beach in the distance. From up-country, where Jan stood, it looked as if nothing had happened.

"Isn't it time for a break yet?" Bea asked, rambling down after Camille to join the others in the lower paddy. After a moment Jan followed them.

"You've got to get into rabbits," Camille explained to Teruko as the two of them helped Marilyn pile dirt up against the retaining wall in the lower paddy. "Rabbits are easy. They're just gonads with long ears. They reproduce like crazy."

"Yeah?"

"It's perfect. You can eat them, use their fur for clothes and their droppings for fertilizer."

"How do the kids feel, eating their pets?" Teri asked.

"Well, it works okay. See, we'll keep the mom and dad as pets. They've got names like Marigold and Marshmallow. But we're giving the babies names like Fluffy Slipper and Dinner. See, I figure it all depends on how you look at them." Camille shrugged and piled another shovelful of mud onto the wall.

Jan rolled her eyes as she caught sight of Teri's drawn expression. Teri's squeamishness seemed ridiculous now.

Jan had met Teri when Jan had moved to Hawaii fourteen years ago to marry Michael. At first she considered Teri part of the local color, simple, perhaps slightly antiquated, a pleasant middle-aged woman, a small wisp of a thing, slow-moving. It had seemed to Jan that all the locals were slow-moving. Teri was Japanese-Hawaian, like Michael, and was considered a local, an insider. Not Jan. Teri was charming, and after a time it was the charm that grated. Now, old annoyances carried over into the new times. They were picked at like scabs. Jan had, over the years, developed the habit of searching out Teri's faults and the habit stuck even now that everything else had changed. Teri doesn't want bunnies harmed, Jan thought. God.

Jan lifted a pile of roots and carried them to the far side of the terrace. The gnarled roots were no good for compost, no good for anything. She tossed them over the side. Bug houses. When the roots hit the ground, two garden roaches scampered out of the bundle. Bea had told Jan that roaches were many times more resistant to radiation than humans were; maybe 400,000 times more, Bea had said. They had both stared down at a roach that was crawling over Bea's worn shoe. Jan had been impressed. She'd started studying the bugs' habits. They are survivors. Good for them, she thought.

When Jan crossed the paddy to pick up another pile of roots she overheard Marilyn talking to Teri. Teri was Marilyn's midwife, and Jan knew she could learn something from their conversations. Besides knowing obstetrics, Teri was privy to gossip and information from town, since she lived down-country and was considered one to be trusted. People had always trusted her. She was discreet.

"Teri," Jan heard Marilyn whisper furtively, "were the soldiers down to your place?"

"Yes, just this morning. They were by your place?"

"Yeah, the tall one came by," Marilyn said, and began chewing the nail on her index finger. Marilyn was pregnant too, showing more than Jan, and the soldiers had been by her house three times before. They made her nervous with all their questions: When was she due? Had she been seriously ill in the past month? Had she considered all her alternatives? As Jan looked over at her, she noticed how Marilyn now looked like a worried old woman. Three years ago Marilyn had been a Lono High cheerleader.

"I really hate it when the soldiers come by," Marilyn said.

Jan interrupted to start the game. "Granola bars."

"Kachi sushi," Teri said.

"Alpha-ghetti," Camille joined in.

"Strawberry Poptarts."

"Cherry jam."

"Apricot jam."

"Apple butter."

"Long's Drugs," Bea said, and she threw down her shovel. Even in the mud she held her stocky body straight, as if she were standing at a podium. "Now listen, ladies. About the soldiers: it's pregnancies they're checking on, and I think you should seriously consider co-operating with them. They're checking for effects from radiation."

Her words slowed the women's work, and Bea, relishing the authority she held because of what she knew, continued. "I understand you all are rather concerned about the soldiers' most recent visits. They approached me about their project. Here. Let me try to explain. You see, it's in their manual to check these things out. Now, don't let their questions disturb you; I've encouraged them to make these inquiries. We can use every bit of information they might collect."

Marilyn listened carefully and her face twitched. Whenever Bea talked about the possibility of side-effects there was the twitch. Most people avoided the subject whenever Marilyn and Jan were within earshot, but particularly around Marilyn. It was assumed that her baby's chances weren't as good as Jan's. Marilyn had been two months pregnant last April; Jan was hardly showing even now.

"Breakfast at McDonalds," Marilyn said, turning away.

"Fresh bran muffins for breakfast," Jan said.

"Wheat flour. I'm almost out of flour," Teri said.

"The country music station," Camille said. "I miss country music. Loretta Lynn. Oh, I loved her singing. It made me swell up inside. It did. It made me...uh..."

"Emote," Bea said.

"Huh?"

"Emote. Sometimes I emote too, listening to music. Particularly listening to Chopin. Frederic Chopin." Then, staring at Jan, who had resumed work, Bea called to the women who were still draining water out into the lower paddy, "Close up the dam now and let's rest, ladies, before Jan knocks herself out."

The women trudged over to sit down against a retaining wall. Thermoses were passed around, cups of peppermint tea were poured, and some women peeled ripe mangoes.

"Real coffee," Marilyn said.

"No," Camille said. "It's just peppermint tea."

15

"I was playing the game," Marilyn laughed.

"Oh, sorry."

Jan retreated several yards up the mountain, far enough so the women's voices could hardly be heard, but still close enough that, if someone had food, they'd share it with her. As she settled onto the bank of dirt, rubbing her belly, she calculated over and over again, trying to figure out when she'd become pregnant. In April? She and Michael, drowning in fear, had grabbed for each other just after the rain. Had she conceived then? Dear God, don't let it be that I conceived in that gruesome moment. But she wondered, if it had been then, maybe the baby would be safer. She calculated the days again.

Jan knew there was no way she'd be able to take care of a deformed child. There was no slack; she had nothing extra to give. Sometimes she wondered if deformed babies would be left somewhere to die now. Not this baby, she had decided; this one will be okay; this one will live. She crept back towards the others and sat down next to Teri.

"Chocolate."

"Chewing gum."

"Kamehameha Bakery."

"Yeah, their dobash cake."

"Let's stop talking about food."

"Okay. Flashlight batteries."

Jan interrupted the game, speaking slowly. "Dr. Bea, what exactly are the soldiers trying to find? They keep after us. They keep asking 'Who is pregnant? Who has miscarried?' Well, I want to know who's had miscarriages, too. Are any women getting pregnant now?" As she raised her voice, it cracked, and her eyes flashed, filling suddenly with angry tears. "What are the soldiers trying to find? Why do they want to know so much? What do they think is happening to us? And what the hell is happening to the soldiers, anyway?"

She felt herself begin to shake. Teri put her arms around Jan's shoulders and Jan straightened up, pulling away from Teri. When they saw Jan stiffen, the other women began to shuffle away from her. Silently, they followed Marilyn's lead, returning to work.

"Frozen yogurt," Marilyn said.

"Double chocolate ice cream," Camille said.

But Bea called after them, "I want to know the answers to Jan's questions. She's right. We need to know what's happening here." Some of the women turned around to listen.

"What is the matter with all of you? Is it the soldiers? You don't want to talk to them?" Bea looked at the few women who had stopped to listen. She picked up her notebook. "I could keep the records instead of the soldiers, but you'd have to help me. I'm trying to keep track of what's happening. What do you think I'm doing here? I'm already keeping track of Jan and Marilyn." She shook her notebook at them. "Bring me the data about your menstruation and any miscarriages, dates and everything. I'll start with this fertility question. If you don't want to co-operate with the soldiers, well, okay. We don't need them. But we do need this information."

"Get what you need from the soldiers, Dr. Bea," Jan muttered, wiping her nose on her sleeve and lifting herself up, just as Bea was settling down with her pen and book to finish recording what she had begun. "They might be able to tell you who's menstruating. They might even be able to tell you when." She turned away from Bea and followed the other women back to work.

It was embarrassing, Jan thought, losing your head in front of the whole group. She hesitated before a new row of plants. The other women were already digging and she watched their thin arms extend and strain with each shovelful of dirt. Their clothing hung loosely on their bodies as they stood in the mud while the paddy began to fill up with water. They all looked dirty and dishevelled. Their thin bodies stuck out of the mud like shards of a broken pot.

Jan wanted to play the game. She caught up with the women setting in transplants. "Toilet paper," she said.

"Nail polish remover," Marilyn said. "I ran out of remover, but I still have some polish. It's just all cracked looking, worse than nothing."

"I'll trade you. Loan me your polish and I'll loan you my remover," Camille said.

"Hand cream."

"Hand soap. We're using laundry detergent now."

"I know how to make hand soap," Marilyn said. "I can teach you."

"Listening to my Loretta Lynn records," Camille said. "I miss the stereo."

"The dishwasher."

"My clothes washer."

"Sitting in the Mahele mall, drinking coffee. Gosh, I miss coffee," Marilyn said.

"You shouldn't be drinking coffee anyway. Not when you're pregnant. That's what Dr. Bea told me," Camille said.

"Shopping at the mall. Shopping at Liberty House," Jan said. "The April sales. End of the Season Clearance."

"You can't miss the April sales yet, Jan," Camille said. "It hasn't been April come and gone."

"But I do." Jan hesitated. "Okay, okay, okay. Furniture polish."

2

First entry of a notebook kept by Dr. Bea Williams:

September 10, Mahele, Kaane, Hawaii

Okay. I do what I can now. I'm a scientist. I do science. But there is little hard data available and actualities no longer emerge as facts, something to rely on. They ooze out.

Still, I do what I can.

We have entered what I like to think of as the new times. Before last April, island life was sustained by a network of interdependencies off-island. Planes brought in most everything we needed—food, medicines, newspapers—and five months ago we were cut loose. Whether it was war or an accident, it amounts to the same for us. The morning plane from Honolulu that delivered our breakfast rolls never landed.

Now each household maintains its own inventory, and with the long tradition of hoarding that prevails, no one acknowledges that some goods are still available, yet severe deprivation has not been evident either. However, most medical supplies are definitely no longer available. There are a mere thirty more doses of morphine left in the hospital, and no more disposable diapers.

Frankly, I had counted on annihilation. The presence of a satellite tracking station here on Kaane, up on Halepele, comforted me. Tourist brochures described it as a research center, a center for the study of volcanoes and silversword plants, but with army personnel trekking up and down between the harbor and the center, we all knew better. We trusted that, if there was a war, the station was targeted and we would all die. The end. It was an article of faith for most of us.

But no.

Perhaps a strategist miscalculated, or maybe there was a power failure in a missile launcher. Whatever. There was no plunge into winter, no second round, and no rescue operation. The changes came slowly.

Sometimes I find I whine.

During the first two weeks we had unseasonably heavy rains, which the local army personnel braved, patrolling the streets on this side of the island, bellowing into megaphones, warning people to stay inside to minimize their possible exposure to radiation. Between downpours their voices, amplified by the bullhorns, echoed in the empty streets like a huge animal's braying. After performing their duty the soldiers scrambled back into their shelter, hoping that the exposure they'd experienced wouldn't be fatal.

Whole families died during those first weeks, one by one, children quicker than the adults. No help was available. Later I tried to trace the pattern of what appears to be radiation sickness, which I presume came from fallout in the rain, to figure out from which direction the fallout is coming—from North America or Asia or both. The results are inconclusive.

People in the Kalawao resort area on the other side of the island—the only populated area on the western side—apparently became ill almost immediately. There were reports from Kalawao that the tourists became frenzied. Illness swept through their hotel complexes. The soldiers didn't make it over that way until it was too late to warn them to stay indoors. According to the reports, piles of trash and the dead bodies told the tourists' story; they had filled the bars and emptied the shops of liquor but the drinks didn't last. I suspect toward the end it would have been difficult to distinguish alcohol poisoning from radiation sickness. After the debauch, they crawled back to their hotel rooms to die, just as the locals on our side of the island began coming out, trying to survive.

The local people now stay clear of tourist areas, and they wield rifles when strangers come looking for food. Apparently, rumors of this have circulated among the few surviving tourists and they keep their distance no matter what the cost.

That was in April, and we are now into September. Decisions must be made. We need to gain a perspective, an understanding, and this is precisely what I can contribute; a new science for the new times, a new data base.

After all, I am a doctor and there are precious few of us still alive on Kaane. Several doctors lived over by Kalawao, and I suppose they are now dead. I am the only woman doctor here, always have been, and perhaps that accounts for my unconventional methods, or perhaps it is my interest in research rather than in the practice of medicine that affords me a slightly different perspective. Nevertheless, I have consistently been most conscientious, particularly in my record keeping.

I must admit, lately I seem to be losing that professional edge. I am overworked and I have so few supplies and no one gets better. However, now I do have an assistant, Teruko Masaoka. She is fifty-eight years old, weighs no more than eighty-five pounds, and has short, black hair cut in neat, straight lines around her small face. She is tiny, but she is nevertheless heroic. Teri learned what she knows from her mother, who was a midwife. Her knowledge is rich in practicalities, short on theory. Most important, she is considered a local, someone to be trusted, although she was born in Japan. She draws upon a body of knowledge passed among midwives, midwife to midwife, mother to daughter. In fact, Teri learned more about obstetrics at her mother's knee than I learned in med school. Her mother taught her invaluable techniques for dealing with difficult births. Since April every birth has been complicated, with most pregnancies ending early in miscarriages or stillbirths.

I am the one who still handles the forceps.

I, in fact, have lived on Kaane nearly as long as Teri, but I am still not considered a local.

Teri is the trusted friend of most of my patients, and admirably suited to serve as midwife. Now only seven women under my care are still with child, but they are scattered between Lono and Mahele and, being without a car, I need Teri. I used to own a Caddie. I loved that car, but it does not operate now. The women trust Teri; she bears their grief. Even Jan Ito, who is, by the way, the most bristly woman I've ever met, trusts Teri.

Data:

Seven women pregnant on the eastern side of the island. Blood pressure, temperature and fetal development to date on my prenatal care patients: all normal.

Teri's efforts aren't limited to medical care; she was the one who organized the first collective farming project, getting some twenty women together to build up new paddies so we can grow taro up-country. We are growing the food that was once the local population's staple. Several times a week the women work together in the paddies and often, during these work periods, information is exchanged that I hope to profitably collect and record.

The small and dwindling group of soldiers stationed here, who were caught on the island in April, will be contributing information for this record inadvertently. They are outsiders, trying to be important, trying to do a job in a community that they have never understood. They have this manual issued by the Army and they adhere to it slavishly. They have become the butt of the local people's anger. They insist on snooping about, carrying on seemingly official business. At the moment they are trying to conduct a census, a task that was outlined in their manual. I have encouraged them. However bothersome, they do gather information that might prove useful.

By maintaining a record I hope to provide ourselves and any future survivors with a history of the new times. Those who assume the worst scorn my interest in history. Admittedly, my professional prognosis is not encouraging, but there have been other times that people supposed were the end, and I feel nothing is gained by presupposing the worst. As a human being living on what could be a scarcely populated planet now, I am convinced that we might prosper again. Therefore my work—

everyone's work—still has meaning.

However, emergency conditions are not conducive to scientific research and study. Night falls, and fires must be built if one is to eat. By day all able-bodied people, even those of us who are not-so-able, are compelled to work. New fields are being planted up-country, and fishing on the beach takes up all spare time. Walking to and from the fields or the beach adds hours to an exhausting work day. Lately I have discovered that I hate walking.

My professional status gains me nothing. No one can pay me or exchange goods for my services. If I demanded payment they would forgo my services. I don't blame them. Their reserves are low and the tools of my work were designed for another time. Drugs are not available. Emergency procedures and blood transfusions are impossible without sterile conditions, electricity and medical supplies. These people don't need me; they need a witch doctor.

Perhaps this calamity is confined to the Pacific region and our isolation is only a temporary effect of limited warfare. Perhaps an accident or volcanic action occurred and only the Hawaiian chain is affected. Perhaps the military has a rescue plan and they are only waiting until the radiation levels are reduced. If so, then we need only to last.

But, in the meantime, our island community has been transformed by adversity and all normal patterns of interaction have been simultaneously transformed. As a doctor with a bent for research, my bias is toward data collection and my scientific skills are restricted to the health disciplines. Yet, I also want to record my observations of psychological and social developments on Kaane, as faithfully and as objectively as I am able, for posterity.

3

Teri motioned Jan to the edge of the taro paddy, away from the other women. "How's Michael doing?" she asked. "Koken worries about him."

Jan shrugged. "He's the same. Still not talking."

"Isn't it strange?" Teri shook her head. "Not a word?"

"No." Jan turned her back to start work again, then hesitated. "Well, that's not exactly true, Teri. Two weeks ago he did say something. He said, 'Shit, we're out of toilet paper.' I guess that counts. That's talking."

Teri smiled. "Yes. I guess that is."

"Teri, he's not the only one."

Teri leaned on her spade. "He's the only one you have to live with."

"I can live with it."

"I didn't mean to upset you. I'm sorry I asked about him."

"I'm not upset. I'm just sick of this business. Everyone makes such a fuss over it. So what if he doesn't talk? What if, one by one, all the men stop talking? We'll get our work done in peace and quiet." Jan pushed her hair off her brow. "Listen Teri, he's depressed. Who isn't depressed? I'm depressed."

"Koken too, of course. Me too," Teri said. "But we can talk. I just thought, it must be very hard on you, Michael not talking."

Jan cut her off. "We're fine," she said, and stepped up onto the retaining wall. She didn't want Teri's pity. Michael will talk when he wants to; it's a relief sometimes, she thought. Anyway, what was there to talk about?

As she stood on top of the retaining wall Jan could see her two young sons coming up the path toward the paddy, pulling their loaded wagon. She watched them trying to manoeuvre it, Steven's large frame directing it, Tomi's short body alternately pushing it and bobbing alongside it. She turned back to Teri. "There's Steven and Tomi. I have to go. See you next week." She hurried down the path to meet her sons.

"Hi Mommy," Tomi said when she reached them. Tomi threw his arms around her legs and as she bent down to hug him, she looked over to Steven.

Steven was twelve. He hated being touched, and since April his hard edge had sharpened. He looked more like her than Tomi did, particularly now that he was almost adolescent. His complexion was light, and there was a streak of red in his straight dark hair that had been bleached by the sun. But Tomi, only six years old and small for his age, took after Michael with his thin eyes, dark skin, and straight, black hair that stuck out like a new broom if Jan cut it too short. Tomi still had a tight, round belly and dimpled hands.

"Wait till you see this stash, Mommy," Tomi said. "We brought lots more food this time, gobs of food. We got this wagon loaded up with oats and stuff."

Jan pulled the blanket back from the top of the mound on the wagon. The bags of oats were stashed into new brass pots. Crystal glasses were wrapped carefully in with the packages of raisins, towels, and rice. Jan inspected the wagonload. "Good work, boys. How was the fishing?"

"Didn't catch a thing," Steven said, and kicked the dirt.

"Nothing but seaweed," Tomi sulked.

"Seaweed is something," Jan said.

"I hate seaweed."

"Well, you don't have to eat it tonight. Look at all this stuff."

"There's no meat," Tomi said. He grinned and elbowed his big brother, his whole cheek wrinkling up around a wink.

"Shut up, Tomi," Steven said.

Jan whispered, "Let's get this stuff out of here before someone sees it."

They turned the wagon around and pulled it back down the path. Once they reached the road they could move quickly. Still, it would take them an hour to reach the house. They took turns pulling the wagon.

Jan was proud of this wagonload. It had been her idea. Last April, hunched over in her basement, she had summed things up; there were to be new rules. So, after two weeks, even before the soldiers gave the 'all clear', she'd packed the family up and they'd driven through the empty streets, down to Mahele. The shopping malls were deserted. Several stores had been looted. A few were burnt out. The family crept through the department store's broken, glass doors.

She had Michael back the car into the mall and then they dragged the boys' wagon up and down the aisles of one store and then another. She and the boys had loaded up the wagon, and again and again they had gone back for more: canned meat, rice, oven mitts, caviar, wine, thread. Michael's office was in a building with a basement. They drove back and forth between the mall and that basement cache. Michael had protested. He said that friends of his owned some of the stores in the mall; he'd even worked in that mall at one time.

"Do you want us to pick another mall? We could go clear over to Kalawao Mall—steal the stuff from a store where you don't know the owner," Jan had said, drumming her fingers on the car's hood.

But Michael shook his head. Already he had been getting quiet. In the end, he hauled whatever Jan loaded onto the wagon. The boys squealed, ransacking the toy department in one store, and moving on to grab model boat kits and airplanes at the hobby store. Jan, on the other hand, had systematically considered their new situation; she filled boxes with fuel starter, fabrics, and blankets, and took one of almost everything from the hardware store, knowing that things eventually break down.

When she was sure she had taken what her family needed she had hesitated. Tableware. She could get new dishes. The best. Liberty House was badly stocked, she decided after surveying the shelves. She decided she should go to the other side of the island, toward Kalawao, to ransack the wealthy tourist boutiques.

The day after their trip to town, she got ready. She had tried to fill the tank of the car herself, the owner of the station near Lono having deserted his garage without locking the tanks. But the pump didn't work, so she calculated the distance again and decided to risk it, figuring she had just enough gas to get there and back. She set out with a gun lying on the front seat next to her.

In Kalawao the shops were empty and she met no one. A

shadow scurried away down one of the large, airy corridors of a hotel as she passed by, but that was all she saw. She had expected something more, some style from the wealthiest people on Kaane, at least that they would continue wind surfing, but there was nothing, no one playing on the water, only a terrible smell. She returned home with two sets of Royal Doulton china and some sterling silverware.

When the soldiers announced that it was safe to go outdoors for short trips, everyone started looting the stores. Evidently the police had signed off too, more or less permanently, and the soldiers turned a blind eye to the looting, afraid to cross the locals. Jan's neighbors, Alex and Charlotte Campbell, had gone into Mahele and had taken whatever they could carry, and Alex was a police officer himself. But by then Jan already had everything she needed, at least everything she could store. She had enough dry food stuff for almost a year, she had figured, and lots of things she never dreamed she'd own.

"Isn't this great, kids?" Jan said, looking over her shoulder at the wagon load she was pulling, as they climbed up toward Lono.

"What's great?" Steven said.

"That we have this stuff. We'll have rice for dinner."

"Oh, that. Great," Steven said. "It's my turn to pull, Mom."

Half-way up from the taro paddy to the house Tomi began complaining. His feet hurt, he said. He was hungry. "Mom, can I have a cookie?" he bleated.

"We don't have any cookies," Jan said.

"Can't we look in the wagon?"

"I know there aren't any cookies. They were all gone a month ago. Let's play the game," she said.

"Chocolate cookies," Tomi said.

"Chanel perfume," Jan said.

"Cookies," Steven said.

"Lemon cake," Jan said.

"Chocolate cookies," Tomi said.

"Tofu," Jan said, and grinned at Tomi. "Now it's your turn, Steven."

"Chocolate cookies," Steven hissed. "I want them now."

Jan's temper flared. "Forget cookies," she growled, but Steven had already turned his back to her. "Oh, forget the game," she said. "Let's just get home and you can have dinner."

"I want cookies," Tomi whimpered, looking first at his big brother and then at Jan.

"Tomi, forget about cookies," she begged him, putting her hand on his shoulder.

"Mommy, can I get a pet instead?" Tomi asked her.

Jan groaned. "A pet. How the hell do you think we can keep a pet?" But she hesitated. "How about rabbits, Tomi?"

She admired her home from the driveway as they pulled the wagon up to the front door; it looked inviting, safe. She swung the front door open. Inside, the house looked almost perfect. The sun, coming through the stained glass window, lit up the brass pots filled with dried flowers and shone on the delicate china tableware. Her dining room table was already set as if a formal dinner was to be served. She set the table every night after the dishes were washed so the last rays of sunlight were caught through the cut crystal glasses as she polished them. Sometimes they were prisms separating the light into spots of bright color.

Jan loved the colored spots. She had never had crystal before, and never before had she cared so much about fine things. When she and Michael were first married they had very little money and had squirrelled away whatever money they could for a down payment on a house. After they had bought the house she had had the two babies. Then dishes had to bounce when they hit the floor, and they had to be safe in the dishwasher. The dishwasher didn't work now, and Jan chuckled, thinking back on their plans. It was a grim new laugh that stuck in her throat. If we'd waited until last April, she thought, we could have taken the house just like I took this crystal, but back then we thought we were being so clever, planning for the future. She looked over the table and blew a few specks of dust off a silver spoon. The boys finished unloading the wagon.

"Let's store those oats and raisins in the microwave, Tomi. Steven, give him a hand. He can't reach that. Hey, check for bugs first," she said. "Put that crock on the tiles by the fireplace. Are there glasses in that?"

Steven shook his head, no.

She followed them into the kitchen, clucking at them about each item. Not to be broken. Not to be spilled.

"Mom, we still have a couple of hours before it's dark. Can Tomi and I go hunting?" Steven asked, putting the pot down on the counter.

"What is that thing?" Jan asked him. "A rice cooker?"

"Yep," Steven replied.

Jan chuckled. "What could I have been thinking? An electric rice cooker?"

"Please, Mom. Can't we go now?" Steven insisted.

"Sure. Run along. Dinner won't be ready for a while."

The two boys tumbled over each other rushing to the door. "Would you watch it?" Steven hissed at Tomi. They grabbed the gun that was kept just inside the door.

"Steven, don't let Tomi use that thing, and you be careful with it too," Jan said. She shook her head. Even the kids near her grandparents' farm hadn't been allowed to use guns.

"An electric rice cooker. Imagine," Jan mumbled in the silence the boys left behind them. "What was I thinking?"

Last April, when Jan and her family emerged from their basement it hadn't occurred to her that the electricity wasn't going to go back on. The workers will repair the system, she had thought. It had seemed impossible that things had changed for good. In her yard everything was as it had been. The plumeria had blossomed. A soft rain was falling, as she had stepped out into the yard for the first time in two weeks. Rain still felt wet. That was just over five months ago, but since then time had come unstuck, no longer attached to events and fixed patterns.

Well, at least I didn't waste my time with cars, Jan thought, and stuffed the rice cooker in the cupboard. Cars hadn't lasted. New models with automatic starters never started again. Old cars ran low on oil. Any breakdown was permanent, since the repair shops were closed and parts couldn't be found. Then, what fuel could be manually pumped out of the tanks was quickly used up.

"Cars," Jan said to herself. "Cadillacs. Jeeps. Chevy vans..." She had tried to play the game alone before. It never worked. She moved around the kitchen, fondling the brass pots. Quality pots, the best enamal pots. Her hands paused at the teak knife rack. Isn't this an impressive collection of knives it holds? Jan laughed to herself. I could become a butcher with good knives like these, if only I could get my hands on some lovely beef.

When they'd built the house Jan had insisted on a fireplace in the living room. People who grew up on the island weren't accustomed to fireplaces, but Michael had given in. Jan thanked God for that every day now. She hated cooking outdoors. Now, as she bent over to stack the wood, Jan felt the baby kick. It's five months along, she calculated. It must be, to kick that strong. A big baby, extraordinarily big... She moved quickly over to the table, picked up a crystal glass, and held it up to the light. She had found ways to stop thoughts before they went too far. She focused on something immediate. The glass sparkled in the light of the setting sun, but she could not make it cast a spot of color.

Still, I'm not showing much yet, she thought, looking down at her abdomen. She wished she were bigger. With her last two pregnancies she had been big by five months. Funny how much it mattered to me during my first pregnancy—how big I got. She smiled, thinking back. Even after the first birth she'd felt huge and clumsy. She had cried when she realized she wouldn't fit into her normal clothes before returning from the hospital after Steven had been born. She had looked in the mirror with horror, her jelly-belly, she called it, hanging loose where the baby had been. None of her clothes fit. She had despaired then, or she'd thought it was despair, but it had really been such a tiny emotion. Now she shook her head, remembering Steven had been a baby.

Lighting the fire distracted her. She placed the grill over the flames, and lifted the kettle of water onto it. She never wasted this heat. Jan longed for enough hot water for a warm bath, even to give the kids a hot bath. Did anyone get clean in a lukewarm tub? she wondered. She was sure she'd be able to get her clothes clean if only they had enough hot water. Their new linens and clothes had already yellowed. If she could get the generator fixed she would have hot water, she figured, and wondered if she could fix it herself.

Satisfied that dinner was underway, Jan ran her hands down

her sides. She had grown to love largeness in her body. She was a sizable person, pregnant or not, but while carrying the baby she felt she had much more presence, like a heavy rock that couldn't be moved out of the way. She wanted her body to grow fat; she wanted her body to take up more space.

But Michael still wanted it for love-making. He grunted a request now and then or held out an open palm, closing it slowly while he stared at her. His gesture scared her. He seemed desperate, but on the other hand, it was not as if he pressured her.

She heard him coming in the front door just as she was lifting another pot onto the grill. "Hey, Michael," she called. "I'm in the living room."

"Hey, what have you got there?" she asked. Without saying a word he opened his scarf and showed her his load of fruit, mostly mangoes.

"Bea says the kids will get allergic if we feed them much more mango," she said. He abandoned the load, looking the other way. Jan's voice softened. "Oh, it's fine for today. I'm not saying it isn't. It's fine. They love mangoes. I just mean we have to be careful, that's all."

Without a word he went into the kitchen, took a knife from the rack and started cutting the mangoes into a crystal bowl.

"Could you say something, just so I know you can still talk?" she said.

Michael shook his head, no.

"Okay. Okay. Just checking."

Jan had scorned the women's concerns over so many men becoming silent. Hadn't we always complained that they talked too much? she'd said. But sometimes it was awful, this furious silence. Some men had been completely mute since April. None of the women had been affected like that except for Bea, and it had only lasted for a little while with her. Bea had tried to explain it to them. She told them that it had felt like being at the bottom of a well; any sound you uttered echoed in your ears. Jan resented Bea's explanation, as if Bea was that sensitive. Does Bea think that the rest of us don't mind what is happening? Jan had grumbled. Does Dr. Bea assume the philosophical problems of this predicament have gone over our heads? Well, lots of women are plenty depressed but we still talk, Jan thought. We have to. We're left to clean up. War or no war, food has to be served.

Actually, Jan realized, it is the fighting I've missed most since Michael stopped talking. Jan never fought with women. No matter how mad they got with each other, they never fought. But she and Michael could really get going—a good match. Michael would stomp around and growl at her, but she could hold a grudge that lasted days. Sometimes she'd shout, but her strength was in her stamina. Having knit his dark brow and roughed up his thick black hair so that it stood out, his anger would be spent. He'd be exhausted and defenceless before she had hardly begun, pricking him, nudging him, still trying to win. Before last April they had fought over the kids, over housework, whether she should take an outside job, money, the usual things. It was a break, really. Sharpened one's wit. Then you make up. Have sex.

Come to think of it, Jan thought as she stirred the rice, how come Michael doesn't fix the generator? How come I'm busting myself? He can do it. Michael Ito, she scolded silently, you're becoming a blob, an amoeba. The old rage rose in her, an old style fight in the making.

But when she glared at Michael she noticed how he moved out of the kitchen and curled up on the couch. Her heart sank. Forget it. He's doing everything he can just to be human, let alone mad. He's no opponent. She knew she could bully him, but what was the point? She settled down to keep her eye on the rice over the flame, watching until it boiled.

An hour later the kids came rushing in, screaming and laughing, dragging the carcass of a large dog behind them. "We got him, Mom. Look. We got him!"

"Oh, my God!" Jan groaned.

"I killed it! For meat!" Tomi squealed. "You said you wanted meat. We can make meat pies!"

Jan clapped her hand over her mouth and ran for the bathroom. They could hear her throwing up into the toilet bowl. Tomi looked confused and disappointed.

Michael saw a look of satisfaction cross Steven's face. "Out," he snarled.

Steven glared at his father. "She needs red meat. We got us meat."

"That's why we killed the dog," Tomi said, nodding his head. "Mom said she needed some red meat. We hunted in the bush up the mountain; we only had a few hours, even less. We knew he was up there somewhere. What luck!" He stumbled on his words in the excitement. "The Chinese eat dogs. I read about that, and my friend, Chong, he told me it's true. His family ate some. It's better than nothing."

Steven lifted the carcass so its blind eyes stared into Michael's eyes. "We need meat and this is meat."

Michael looked into the dog's eyes, and then into his son's. He took a step closer to Steven, but Steven didn't move. Michael waited.

Tomi shifted his weight from one foot to the other. "Come on, Steven. Let's take this out and scalp it."

Steven didn't move. Finally Michael shook his head and turned around at the sound of a hiss in the fire. He picked up the spoon and stirred the rice as it bubbled over onto the blaze. Tomi looked back and forth between Steven and Michael, uncomprehending, as Jan emerged from the bathroom, wiping her mouth.

"That's great, kids," she said. She caught Steven still glaring at his father's back.

But then Steven smiled. "Mom, Dad and I can skin him. Once it's cured and cooked you'll think your eating beef. You just lie down until dinner. We can take care of it," he said.

"Sure, Mom. We'll take care of it." Tomi echoed his big brother.

"I thought you said you wanted a pet, Tomi?" she said, ruffling his hair. She bit the inside of her cheek. "Why didn't you just keep the old hound?"

"We need the meat," he told her. "That's what Dr. Bea said, too. You need red meat."

"I'm not eating any pet pie," she said, but she realized it wasn't true; she was hungry for meat. She avoided looking at the dead mutt's eyes. "Is that a basset hound?"

"Ah Mom, just go to bed," Tomi said. "We'll bring some rice in for you when it's done."

"Thanks," she said.

Alone in her room, she crawled into the bed and pulled the eiderdown quilt up to her chin. Cool sheets touched her rough skin and began to warm up as her body sank down into the mattress. The light was fading and the delicate colors lit her dreams. She didn't incorporate into her dreams the sounds her sons made as they worked, knives clicking against each other, the hide ripping as they skinned and hung the dog's carcass out in the carport.

She dreamt of a baby swimming in warm clear liquid. Perfectly formed wide eyes and thin lips whispered unintelligible words.

4

September 14

Notes on island demographics:

Present population of Kaane: 22,000; 10,500 grown women; 10,000 grown men; 1,500 children (16 years of age and under). These statistics are approximations adjusted from the last census to take into consideration the deaths that have occurred in recent months, assuming that nearly all the permanent residents of the Kalawao area are dead and that the surviving tourist population on the island is negligible, perhaps no more than one hundred.

Population of the neighboring islands: unknown.

Notes on depression and the great silences, and a confession:

Is it a crime to respond to the situation? Anti-social to be depressed? Of course, I was temporarily afflicted with speechlessness myself so I understand the phenomenon. What I do not understand is the animosity and confusion expressed by those not afflicted. To be bruised when one is beaten is normal. To show no marks of a beating—that is mysterious.

Take me as an example. When the effects of what we must assume was fallout were first felt I was enormously useful. I must have seemed oblivious to the desperate facts of our situation as I administered pain-killers to the hopeless, antibiotics to the infected, wrapped wounds of a kind I'd never seen before, delivered babies, many of whom were dead or born to dying mothers, and soon we were completely out of supplies. Is this the behaviour of a sick woman? I attempted practising triage to the best of my ability, but relatives of those who were refused specific treatments became murderous. I was being a war hero here, and everyone thought I was on the take. It mattered little.

Before long, with no electricity and very few medical supplies, there was no medical treatment available to fight over; I was as useless as the soldiers. Yet, unlike the soldiers, I failed to find useless activities to pump myself up. So I simply had nothing to say. I fell silent.

The stranger symptom of depression, to my mind, is not the deep silence, but rather the dogged determination manifested in some other people, to produce food, to scrounge out another day's health and light when the next day is so unsure. This stance of determined optimism has been taken by the women involved in the taro project. They have focused on, one might even say that they are obsessed with, production. But there is no cynicism in their efforts. They believe it is to some end.

Their word games relieve the tedium. Occasionally a crevice appears, usually during a moment of reflection, that threatens to become a gulf into which they might plunge to the depths of hysteria. The display of minor hysterical symptoms leads me to wonder if deep sublimation is at the root of all the phenomena. Strong sexual energy can be repressed to produce similar symptoms. Of course, it must be recognized that, given our present circumstances here on Kaane, the symptoms these women manifest suggest a most functional neurosis, to be sure. It would be interesting to see psychoanalytic work done here, but there is no time in the new times.

Small things aggravate the situation. There is no more tobacco or alcohol. I, for one, would kill now for a cigarette. Withdrawal from common drugs and bad habits, under stressful conditions, has been salt on the wounds. Compounding the aggravation is the scarcity of some foods, the closing of the schools, and the necessity of the elderly or even children being forced to move in with other families. Yet, given the collapse of official forms of government regulation of behaviour, the absence of extreme anarchistic behaviour is remarkable.

For my part now, I simply want to protect what I have. Although most of the hospital supplies are depleted, I have my black bag stuffed with small quantities of various medicines, mostly samples that were left behind by sales people who passed through before April. For use as an anaesthetic, I also keep my flask of Cutty Sark. My supplies are not really enough to get most doctors through the day, but I do get by.

Apart from these meagre provisions, I want to protect the few supplies that I have stashed away in larger quantities. I hoarded these even as the drugs and bandages diminished and the number of victims swelled. From a bar in town I confiscated a case of scotch which I use to replenish the flask in my bag. This I have administered to patients sparingly, for instance when an amputation is being performed; six shots for the patient and one shot for me. I have also hidden a half-litre bottle of suspended penicillin to be used only for a more urgent case than any I have yet seen, and I have secured one measly tablet of cyanide.

I cling to these last doses of penicillin as a child to her teddy. Some extraordinary person, more worthy than all the good people who have come to me before, may require it and I will be prepared. But of course no extraordinary person survives; rather, a dreary mass of people. So it always is.

The period of silence was a great purging for me. Once I emerged and joined the living in the task of survival I left grief behind. I left behind illusions of what might have been. I left behind the desire to become a researcher, except such research notes as you find contained in these notebooks, and my desire to one day marry. For now and for the forseeable future, it is my part only to serve and observe. I look on.

Report on the soldiers:

There are approximately fifteen soldiers remaining on the island, presumably stationed here to man the satellite tracking station. The sergeant who died in the explosion, when the station blew up on the third day of the new times, was an idiot, but he was their only local boy. Before last April, being a local meant you got better service in restaurants, more jobs were open to you, you could run for office, and people laughed at even your bad jokes. In the new times it means you are automatically included in the island survival plan. I have lived on Kaane for only twenty-two years. I am not a local. I have to earn my right to inclusion. So do the soldiers.

But their behaviour is cagey and isolationist. Treated by the locals as enemy occupiers, they respond in a cold and efficient manner that renders them pathetically inefficient. They conduct official-like business for no apparent reason. They seem to have no knowledge about what really happened last April. They have provided us with no information regarding the explosion that destroyed the tracking station. In fact, they've provided us with no information at all since their admittedly helpful advice to remain indoors last April. That warning was the death gasp of the old times. If they were to issue a similar warning today they would be ignored if not ridiculed.

Perhaps the scorn heaped upon the soldiers is attributable to the government bureaucrat's mannerisms that they've recently adopted. They shuffle busily around which is, in fact, a vast improvement over their previous tendency to exhibit a strutting, military behaviour. However, neither bureaucratic manners nor military manners are considered good manners in the new times community, since the locals are not in the least interested in being governed, nor are they interested in any further protection the military has to offer.

Because of their isolation the only food available to the soldiers is the food that they confiscate (steal). They must realize that this practice further jeopardizes their standing in the community and consequently minimizes their ultimate chances for survival. Their plight parallels that of the tourists. It is a perilous situation, to be dependent on the local community's goodwill.

Inventory of livestock:
There is a cattle herd on a ranch near Ahupuaa that decreased by 70%, presumably because of radiation exposure. However, using the remnants of that herd, every family willing to maintain a cow has one, and a few surviving bulls service the cows on a rotating basis. Breeding, however, is down and the

number of stillborn cattle and calves with fatal defects is high. The calves born with no hair look like huge baby birds, their veins and organs showing. They both fascinate and repel me. Yesterday a calf was born with two heads, it couldn't lift either of them, and all I could think about was how much my older brother would have loved to see this pathetic thing preserved, like those strange animal fetuses he once dragged me off to see at the county fair. He told me, on that occasion, that this is what happened if you masturbated: your babies would be born strange. Yesterday as I stared at the creature I wondered what the calf's mother had done that was so bad.

Severely birth-defected calves are destroyed. Total number of heads of cattle: 240.

I am keeping a dairy cow myself, even though I live alone. My cow is named Moo-moo.

Proposal to increase the number of livestock:

Koken Masaoka, Teri's husband, is organizing a trip whereby some young men will canoe over to Pua Island on the outriggers. Pua Island is not populated. The military used it for target practice, but wild goats and sheep have survived there; they were spotted with a telescope. While Koken considers himself too old to make the expedition himself, several young men he knows have already volunteered to go and capture some of these animals, bring them back to Kaane, and establish a small herd, which would provide an additional source of protein. Also, some people have designs on the wool for knitting.

Number of live births since April:

Eighty. A pattern was observed by some hospital nurses who continued to attend births after April: the mothers who were close to full-term in their pregnancies last April delivered healthy newborns more than 50% of the time; the others delivered stillborn or premature infants. Because no backup facilities were available, most of the premature babies failed to survive.

By June the number of live births decreased substantially. Most pregnancies were aborting in the first trimester. Since July no live births have been reported. The irregularities observed in the fetuses that are spontaneously aborting are due to chromosomal breakage in a sperm or egg cell. However, deformities might also occur even when the sperm and egg cell are genetically normal if radiation kills specific cells in the developing embryo during the first three months. The pregnancies most at risk from this effect—damage *in utero*—are now entering their third trimester.

I have two patients in this latter category. Marilyn Nakatsura's baby is certainly at risk of having been damaged *in utero*, because she conceived in March. I suspect Jan Ito also falls within this high-risk category, but we do not know precisely when she became pregnant. If she conceived in the latter part of April or even in early May and, for reasons unknown, did not abort in the first trimester, then her child could be the first baby born in the new times.

5

The dog carcass was suspended on an S hook, hung from the ceiling in the carport. Covered with a burlap bag to protect it from scavengers and insects, it was almost indistinguishable among the ropes and pails and pieces of hose that hung behind it on the wall. The soldier, as he wandered around the house and through the carport to get to the front door, accidentally bumped the carcass with his rifle, and it was still swinging back and forth and around on its hook when the soldier knocked at the front door.

The family woke up to banging on the door. Tomi was the first to make it to the door. As he opened it, he saw the soldier and hollered down the hall to the others, "They're here. Come on guys, they're back!" Then he opened the door wide and, coming thigh-high to the soldier whose big gun was now propped up against the door jamb, he shrugged his shoulders and giggled.

The soldier cracked a smile at the sight of the child. "Sonny, are your folks home?"

"Sure are. They're coming."

Jan grabbed her bathrobe and came into the front hall. She leaned against the door jamb, and stood casually about a foot from the soldier's face. Looking up, she smiled. "Well, look who's home from the war. I don't believe I've met you, mister. You just arrived on the little oasis?"

The soldier eyed her nervously, looking down at her sarcastic smile; he had at least six inches on this woman.

"What victories do you want to report to us this morning, Mr. Soldier?" Jan continued. "Have we caught up with the enemy yet?"

The soldier tried to control the twitch in his eye. He was determined not to rub it. "Lady, I'm sorry if I woke you. I just have a few questions, if you'd be kind enough to co-operate."

"Go ahead. Let's see if I can help," she said and picked up his gun, swinging it over her shoulder. He grabbed it back and held it at his side.

"We are taking a census. We need to know how many women are pregnant and how far along they are." He pulled a clip board with a sheath of paper on it from his pack. "How many women of child bearing age reside in this household, lady?"

"None."

"None besides yourself, ma'am?" His eyes rested on her belly. She looked down at it herself, and then looked him right in the eye.

"None period, soldier. I'm older than I look, a lot older. You need to know anything else?"

"Well, ma'am. This is very important. We're trying to protect your health and the health of the unborn, you understand. It's for your own good. It's very important..."

Jan cut him off. "If I need any more of the army's protection I'll let you know. Right now I can't afford it. I've got my hands full here, as you can see. But I wish you all the best, soldier." She tried to close the door on him, but he pushed it open again.

"You must co-operate, lady," he hissed, red-faced. "You do realize we are under martial law."

"Oh no, I'm sorry. I didn't know that. I thought the government had blown itself up. So you've heard from them, have you? And they declared martial law?"

"I'll ask you again, lady..."

"I answered you already, soldier boy. No one of child-bearing age lives here. You can search the house for tampons if you'd like," and she gestured him to come in.

The soldier flushed, looked again at her bulging abdomen, scribbled something on his clip board and glared. "Very well, madam. Good day." He turned on his heel.

"So long, soldier." Jan yelled after him before closing the door.

Tomi and Steven were snickering in the next room. "You sure take care of those guys, Mom. Every time," Steven said as she came in.

"Well, I hope you're learning something," she said. "If someone wears a uniform, don't trust them. They want you to believe they're special, that they're not like the rest of us."

44

The boys stared up at her and she shook her head. She was confusing them, going on about things they couldn't understand, but now that she couldn't talk to Michael she'd turned to them. She knew it wasn't fair to them; afterwards she always felt badly.

"Can you believe these guys?" she laughed. "Every day they come by with something new. They act like they won a war. Hey, let's get ourselves some breakfast."

"Mom, did our soldiers fight in the war?" Tomi asked.

Jan met his eyes and spoke softly. "We don't have any soldiers, Tomi. These men were the government's soldiers and the government is gone. These guys are unemployed like the rest of us. They just haven't figured it out yet."

"Well, I was just thinking, Mom, if they did fight in this war then maybe they're radioactive. Some kids told me if they are radioactive they'll glow in the dark. Are they? Are they radioactive?"

"Tomi, don't be stupid," Steven said.

"You can always tell the radioactive men," Jan told him. "They are dead."

Tomi winced. Jan saw it out of the corner of her eye, but Steven knocked him on the shoulder and Tomi relaxed.

"Come on, dummy," Steven said. "Let's get the fire going." The two boys took the oats and some pans to the fireplace and began placing the logs for the morning fire. Steven poked around in the ashes to find a small ember. Finding none, he went over to the bookcase, took out a wooden match, struck it and, cupping his hand around the small flame, carefully placed it under a few scraps of kindling.

"Remember the Sugar Frosted Flakes we used to have for breakfast, Steven?" Tomi asked. He reminisced about frosted flakes nearly every morning. "You didn't have to cook them."

"Soon you won't have oats to cook either, so enjoy them, kids," Jan said, standing over the two boys as they tended the small blaze.

"Good. I hate oats," Tomi said.

"And you hate poi, but that's what you better get used to."

Steven looked up at her, imperious. "Never," he said. "We'll hunt wild boar for breakfast. Won't we, Tomi?"

"Well, when you can get it we'll eat wild boar. In between we'll eat poi, not frosted flakes," Jan said, and turned her back to them.

"I want frosted flakes," Tomi whined.

"I want a strawberry tart with whipped cream on top," Jan said, and smiled.

Steven jumped up. "I want a banana split with whipped cream and marshmallow and chocolate syrup."

"I want steak and eggs, and a toasted Danish, and fresh squeezed orange juice, and coffee with real cream," Jan said.

Tomi was quiet again while his brother put water in the pot to boil. He looked at his mother's face and his eyes clouded. He started to cry. Jan looked at him and tried to smile, masking her irritation. "What's the matter, baby?"

"I want frosted flakes."

Jan thought she was going to hit him, but she held her breath and sank down onto the sofa, feeling the heaviness. Tomi was soft. Before the war it made her nervous; now it filled her with rage. He wouldn't survive if he didn't toughen up. Still, she thought, he's only six years old. Why do I have to rub his nose in it all the time?

Jan knew it was impossible to explain it to him. She couldn't make him understand that they were in between times, that it was always the last time for frosted flakes, last chance to get fine china, to find plastic toys. She had grieved over their last bowl of flakes herself. And Michael had grieved over the last roll of toilet paper. And the last... Tomi was so young. Still, he needed to be tough. Jan wanted to give him some of her own toughness, but the harder she was on him the weaker he became.

She took her youngest into her lap. "Hey, Tomi, let's play the game while Steven cooks up some of this great breakfast." Tomi curled up on what was left of her lap while Steven added oats to the boiling water. Jan felt the warmth of Tomi's body. She thought, I want to memorize the feel of him in my lap with my arms around him. But the feeling was gone too quickly.

"Frosted flakes," Tomi said.

"Coffee," Jan said.

"A spear," Steven called over to them. "A good spear."

"Marshmallow Robots Cereal," Tomi said.

It was Jan's turn. "Fresh squeezed orange juice. No. Fresh ice-water."

"New running shoes," Steven said.

"Snowcones. Hey!" Tomi squealed and jumped out of Jan's lap. "I felt the baby kick, Mom! This time for sure that's what I felt."

"That's right. That's what it was," she said, rubbing her abdomen. "Hey, Steven, do you want to feel it? It'll move again in a minute."

Steven came over to her, bashfully putting his hand on her stomach while she guided it to the swell. "See how lopsided my stomach is? That's because the baby is over on this side," she explained. Steven was embarrassed. Too close to puberty, Jan thought. She knew her pregnancy scared him. Everything about sex scared him now. But Tomi, he was still young enough to poke and stare.

"Let me feel it," Michael said. They hadn't noticed that he'd come into the living room, and the sound of his voice nearly threw Jan off the chair.

"Well, listen to that. Today he talks, boys!" she said.

"Hey, Dad. The baby is right here." Tomi took his father's hand and put it on Jan's belly, but the movement had subsided.

"That little guppy went back to sleep, I guess," Jan told them. "Maybe you can feel it later." She looked up at Michael. "Hey, say something else, honey. Tell me what you want to name the baby."

Michael didn't answer. He took his hand away from his wife's abdomen and went over to the fire to check the boiling pot.

"Dad, did you hear Mom getting rid of the soldier?" Steven asked, but Michael didn't respond. He just picked up the ladle and stirred the porridge.

"Michael, did you sleep well?" Jan prodded, moving next to him by the fire, but there was no answer. She turned back to the boys. "Okay, enough talking, guys. You've got chores. Eat your cereal before it burns, and get to work."

Michael ladled out a bowl for her. She took it onto the sun deck, as he and the boys sat down at the table to eat theirs.

Out on the deck Jan felt the warm sun against her face. She gave herself ten minutes to eat and look over the harbor before she would get to work. Today she was planting in the vegetable garden. Only sixteen packages of seed were left. These seeds had to grow, had to get to maturity and produce more seeds. She couldn't afford mistakes; she needed these seeds for trading.

From the deck Jan could see the generator sitting idle below her. She had found the motor last May, she'd got it working and stashed quite a lot of gasoline away for it as well. That was when everyone else was still waiting for the world to be put right, she thought now, once again congratulating herself for having laid claim to the generator. That was smart. No one else had thought to find a generator.

But now the generator was just another dead carcass. It broke down after a month from too much use. She had shared it with the neighbors, showing off, running several lights, even appliances, off the tiny motor. She had learned the hard way with the generator: don't waste and don't share if you can help it. Still, she'd find a way to fix it yet.

From the sun deck she could see the soldier trudging along the road, going down-country to bother the women in Mahele. She looked away to the harbor. It was going to be a good day for working in the garden. The cow's manure could be mixed with the soil now to prepare it for planting later in the week. The last seedlings she had planted had burnt off. This time she would make screens to protect them from getting scorched by the hot sun. She caught Michael's eye as he stared at her through the open window. Why didn't he figure out how to fix the generator? Her anger rose again, but then, just as quickly she decided, no, better leave him be.

Sometimes Jan worried that Michael would go crazy and kill her. What if all the talking welled up inside him and came out as one murderous cry? And what if he was holding a knife just then? That had happened in a couple of households over the summer. The husband or wife just snapped and did in themselves and their whole family. Ugly tales like that scurried across the island. Last week a thirteen-year-old girl took a gun and shot her mother, her father, her four-year-old kid sister, and then put the gun to her own head. Rumor had it that she'd done a terrible job. The mother and kid sister bled to death over several days. Camille had told Jan that one, told her in whispers.

When Michael caught Jan's eye he ducked back into the bedroom, dressed hurriedly, and left for down-country. Jan turned away and stared at the railing, watching a sleek green gecko stalk a cockroach. The roach got away.

Jack, the soldier who had been to Jan's house that morning, was having a hard time as he wound his way down the road, back to the barracks. All his strength was gone, but he hadn't felt bad earlier in the morning. No, he had felt pretty good when he woke up, once he finally got his feet down next to his cot. He decided he wasn't going to make any more house calls that day.

I just can't understand these people here, Jack thought, plodding down the mountain. We shouldn't have let the sergeant die. Maybe he could have told us what's going on in these people's heads.

The sergeant had been the only one in the troop who came from Hawaii, not that he knew any other locals on Kaane, not that he felt any attachment to anyone. Still, he'd tell stories about local people, people he'd known as a kid, people his parents knew. Jack wondered if he was feeling guilty about the sergeant.

Right after they'd been cut off last April, the sergeant informed his troop that they were going to blow up the satellite tracking station. It was one of several strategic sites on the island, he had said. Everything had to be cleaned up. He didn't want the enemy to get hold of that equipment. The soldiers wondered if their sergeant had gone mad; there was nothing of consequence on Kaane; they'd been wasting their time there for years. Still, the sergeant kept making these plans, and the other men were sure that civilians would get killed if the sergeant had it his way. That's why no one pointed the sergeant's mistake out to him, up there on Halepele. Instead, they let him blow himself right off the mountain. Later they missed his stories.

No, Jack admitted. He didn't feel guilty about the sergeant. It was that lady; that's who had made him feel so bad. There was no reason for her to be so mean. Who the hell was she, anyway? he thought. Maybe the sergeant had been right to hate the people here. Maybe the soldiers shouldn't have let him blow himself up.

49

6

Steven worked in his room for a week, grinding down an old bit of metal he'd found in his mother's pants pocket. He had realized he would need a spear; the gun wasn't going to last forever, already they were low on ammunition. The bit of metal would make a perfect spearhead, once it was sharpened and strapped onto a pole. Steven had been practising hurling shafts, hunting down the few stray cats that lurked in the bushes near his house. His aim was good. When the spearhead was ground down and sharpened, he went out hunting. Within just a few hours he had skewered a mongoose. After that he considered himself a real hunter.

Steven was sure he was good enough, strong enough, old enough that he should be allowed to go to Pua Island with the older boys. He could paddle a canoe. He could learn. He was strong. The expedition was just days away. If Koken could be convinced Steven should go, then neither Michael nor Jan would stop him. Good old Koken. Koken was like a grandpa to Steven, tall, husky from years of heavy work, maybe too old to make the trip himself but still a bear of a man. Steven would take Koken's place on the boat, and Jan wouldn't be able to stop him.

As it turned out, Jan didn't even try.

Steven carried his weapon across his shoulder the morning when he, Tomi, and Michael set out, walking down the mountain to meet the other hunters on Pali Beach. Jan had got up early to wave goodbye to them. They left before the sun had risen and by the time they had reached the foot of the mountain the blue of the early morning darkness made the silvery cane stalks look like a jungle. Rodents and birds freely made their homes in the cane fields, now that the fields were no longer sprayed with insecticides. Tomi saw a mongoose slink across the road and he whipped out a slingshot and a rock from his pocket, but by the time the sling was loaded the mongoose was nowhere to be seen. Steven, however, was no longer interested in spearing mongoose.

"Tomi," Michael said and put out his hand to take the slingshot. Tomi was startled at the sound of his father's voice. "Your stones are too big," he told the boy. "Smaller, round ones go further—more accurate too."

The rest of the way down the mountain Michael and Tomi kicked stones up as they walked, looking for the perfect round ones. Steven did not look at the ground. He walked straight, eyes ahead. Of the three, he was the only one making the crossing to Pua Island in the canoes. Those who made the crossing had to be quick to lasso the animals; they wanted to bring at least a dozen of them back to Kaane alive. The one animal that would be killed—the one that they would roast and eat on their expedition—Steven wanted to be the one to make that kill.

By the time they reached the beach it was mid-morning and the men were already loading the boats with ropes, traps, food, and water. The young men who would be making the crossing were checking that there was enough food. The older men envied the younger ones the adventure. It was less than twenty miles to the deserted island, but the waters over there were tricky, and the extent of contamination on Pua was unknown. It couldn't be too bad, they reasoned; the sheep were still alive. They'd been sighted with a telescope. Still, the men were grateful when the soldiers offered to loan their geiger counter to the young men who were making the crossing.

Four soldiers were hanging around at the edge of the group. They seemed to be tending the fire, not talking. A pot of coffee on the coals was kept brewing and they passed around a few mugs whenever the fresh pot was done. The coffee was accepted, but when Steven saw it he wondered where the soldiers had stolen the coffee grounds.

The sun was getting high and the sand was getting hotter. By noon it would be too hot; the sand would burn their feet when it slipped under their rubber thongs, and the young men wanted to get off. Banter flew back and forth as they lashed the animal cages down into the huge outriggers. Some of the men who had come to see the expedition off were unpacking camping gear, intending to spend the night on the beach after the boats were launched.

Steven kept close to the boat. He didn't know the others who were going, since they were all several years older than him, and he wanted to be sure he wasn't left behind. He watched the soldiers standing outside the group, and studied their faces from a distance. He couldn't make sense of their shuffling. They seemed awkward and nervous, yet they were the ones who had guns. When Michael had drained his coffee mug, Steven grabbed it to return it to the soldiers. He approached the tall one, the guy who had been at his house the other day. Steven couuld see that the soldier didn't recognize him. He looked down at the sand as he handed over the mug. "Here, sir. It's finished."

Jack took the mug and smiled at the boy who didn't look up. "Thanks, sonny." Steven just stood there, digging his toes deeper into the sand.

"Can I pour you some more?" Jack offered.

But just then Steven turned around quickly. "No sir. Thanks," he said over his shoulder as he darted back towards the boat, kicking up sand as he ran. Jack brushed the sand off his trousers.

Then everyone was pushing the boats into the calm water, hollering directions at each other, the young men jumping aboard and grabbing their oars. Five boats carrying thirty-six young men started across. Some younger boys climbed up on the cliffs where they could see the outriggers set off and could look out for whales that often played in the channel. No water spouts could be seen today, though. The water and the sky met in a perfect, calm blue, as the last outrigger was pushed off the sand bar. The men who were left behind followed the young boys up to the sand banks. The sun reflected off the waves and the men had to shield their eyes with their hands on their brows. The outriggers looked like birds skimming the water, moving over the waves quickly as the paddles were dipped in unison again and again.

Koken sighed, proud for having organized such an expedition. Even if nothing came of it, the sight of the boats was enough. He knew Teri would be proud of him, too. Michael patted his friend Koken on the back, and Koken brought his large dark hands together.

"You want to get some fish?" Koken asked.

Michael nodded, and followed the lumbering old man down the

beach. Tomi trotted after them. They spent the rest of the morning fishing, setting out their catch to dry, and harvesting seaweed to placate Jan. Then all afternoon they looked for shells and fish in the black volcanic rocks that jutted into the water making reefs and small ponds that teamed with sea animals.

That evening they would get together with the other men who had not made the crossing, and they would make a big fish stew. They would sleep under the Pali so they could be there when the boats returned in the morning. And when the boats returned—that's when there would be a real party. That's when there would be meat. Now the afternoon spread out over the long, hot beach.

September 18

Camille's tea recipe:
Use one tablespoon of dry mint leaves for every three cups boiling water. Let it steep for five minutes. This tea is particularly good for mild stomach upsets.

Garlic cure:
With the shortage of medicines, garlic, which is known to be a mild antibiotic, effective in fighting colds and minor infections, has been planted in large quantities on the island. The women planted a crop of single cloves above the taro paddies, and these cloves, in time, will produce an abundance of bulbs. Unfortunately garlic has a very long growing period.

A prayer remembered:
"Forgive, O Lord, my little jokes on Thee
And I'll forgive thy great big one on me."
Robert Frost

7

Up-country, Jan hoed in her back garden, tracing two short rows into the dirt. Carefully she deposited one seed into each small hole, a quarter-inch deep. She patted the soil over the top. One seed at a time; the process took on the sensation of a religious ritual. Expectation, hope. Another seed. Water poured over the dirt. First it pooled. Then it seeped into mud. Careful not to pour too much water on. Not to wash away the seed. Another seed. More soil.

The boys would be gone at least until tomorrow, perhaps longer, and Jan counted on these two clear days to be alone. That morning she had moved through the empty house, tasting the solitude as time spread out around her. Her body seemed to move more gracefully in the solitude, and she had watched the curtains undulate slowly in the breeze that came through the window. She had plans for the day, building the frames that would provide shade for the seedlings, but there was no hurry to begin. She boiled more tea leaves and sat, staring into the fire and then out the window, down the mountain to the ocean where translucent lights played back and forth between the water and the sky.

When she began to work the sun was hot on her back, but she relished the warmth. It went over her spine into her head and it was wonderful, making her feel confident that this time the seeds would grow. After planting most of the seeds she straightened up, stretched her mouth wide open, and poured the water that was left in the can into her mouth. It overflowed, the water dripping down her chin, making rings around her bulging abdomen.

Jan was stretching worn bed sheets over the wood when she noticed Camille coming down the path into the back gully. Camille was dressed in a short polyester knit muumuu, pink with a bit of stiff ruffle around the hem. Her face looked pinched. She chewed her nails even as she walked down the path. Last January, at a New Year's party, Jan had wondered why Ralph's wealth never showed on Camille. He wore linen suits, certainly not a man's equivalent to this pink muumuu. Since April the differences between Camille and Ralph had become even more marked. Ralph had become silent, for which everyone was grateful because when he did speak it was bitter and ugly; Camille still twittered.

"Well, beautiful, how are you?" Camille greeted Jan.

"What a surprise," Jan said.

"Look at you, out here in the sun, girl. What are you up to? You're lucky you haven't got sunstroke yet."

Jan said nothing for a moment. She put down the frame she'd been holding.

"Now what is that contraption?" Camille asked.

"It's a frame for the seedlings. I can't afford to have another crop burn off."

"Isn't it God's best miracle, the life of a seed," Camille bubbled.

As Camille marvelled, Jan chafed. She hated bubbling and it surprised her that, while she had always prided herself on her broad-minded attitudes toward religion, her tolerance evaporated whenever she came face to face with Camille.

"There's some tea I can heat up in the house, Camille. You want to stay?" Jan offered. She hoped Camille would not stay, but Camille's head was bobbing yes, and Jan finally smiled.

The two women went into the house, kicking off their sandals at the door. Jan poured the lukewarm tea and handed a mug to Camille. With tea in hand, Camille came to the point immediately. "Did you get wind of the trip our church is taking?" she asked.

"No," Jan said.

"We're organizing a trip to visit the tourists across the island. The reverend is very concerned to see how they are doing."

"Doesn't seem like it's our business."

"It's God's business and that's our business. That's what the reverend says."

"Does he?"

"Would you or Michael be interested in coming along? We're only going to be gone just a few days."

Jan hesitated and then wondered aloud, "Why is everyone so big on adventure lately? The soldiers' trip to Kalawao seems to have killed nearly half of them off; and now there's this trip to Pua Island, and after that you're going back to Kalawao? It's foolhardy. All these adventures..."

Camille was shaking her head. "This isn't adventure. Well, I guess doing the Lord's work is an adventure. But it is not fool-hardy."

"It's none of my business, but I think God's got more sense than to send people over to the other side of the island," Jan said. "Hey, let's talk about something else, Camille. Let's play the game. Horse-radish."

"Oh, Jan. I hate that game. You know, it's really just the people from our church who were planning on going, but since you showed some interest in the church—you remember the prayer meeting—I just thought this would be a good chance for you to get to know everyone. We're all going. The reverend wants to meet you too. He thought it was a good idea to invite you. We've been collecting food to take to the tourists for several weeks now."

Jan did remember the prayer meeting she had attended with Camille. It was last February. That's what Camille is thinking about, that I'm ripe for the picking because I attended her meeting, Jan thought. Last January Jan had taken a part-time job as a cosmetics distributor, and Camille had talked so much about her women's prayer group that Jan had thought it would be the perfect place to make contacts. She had asked Camille if she could attend a meeting, and Camille had enthusiastically agreed to take her, but as soon as Jan arrived she'd realized her mistake. For one thing, none of the women wore make-up, and for another, they spoke in tongues. It gave Jan the shivers. And now Camille thought Jan's interest in her group had been prompted by Jesus, not by Mary Kay Cosmetics.

Jan resolved to end the discussion. "I don't want to go, Camille, and I don't think Michael will want to go either. We're just not interested in that sort of thing."

"But Teri considered coming," Camille objected.

"And she's not even white," Jan finished.

Camille looked stunned at Jan's remark. She didn't raise her eyes to meet Jan's, but Jan saw that her face was red. "I wasn't suggesting that had anything to do with this," Camille spoke firmly.

"There are many committed Japanese Christians on this island as well as in Japan."

It was the most articulate statement she had ever heard Camille utter but, Jan thought, how the hell would Camille know if Japan still exists? Still, Jan didn't want to argue with her. "I only meant, Camille, that I'm surprised you asked Teri, since you said it was just people in the congregation going. Come on, Camille. Let's play the game."

"I need to know if you're coming with us."

Jan hesitated and her hand came to rest on her abdomen. She smiled and patted it. "Camille, I can't possibly go, not in my condition."

"Oh, of course," Camille conceded. Jan supposed Camille was also regretting the visit now. "I thought really, maybe it would be too much for you. But I did want to invite you, to let you know you are welcome, just in case you felt up to it."

"Well, talk to Michael about it if you can," Jan added. She felt embarrassed. She always went too far with Camille.

"I will. And what about the boys?"

"No. I really think they are too young, Camille. I'd appreciate it if you didn't even mention it to them."

"Whatever you think best."

They finished their tea and Jan excused herself, saying she had to get back to work. Camille asked if she could help Jan with any lifting. "Everyone's so worried that you work too hard," she said.

"It's light work," Jan said.

Camille smiled. "Is there anything you'd like to contribute to the food baskets? For the tourists?" she asked.

"Oh, yes. I guess I might have something." Jan walked over to her cupboard. She opened it carefully so Camille wouldn't see the whole of its contents, and took out a can of pea soup. Pangs in her chest made her hesitate; it was their last can of prepared soup, but Camille would not leave empty handed and Jan wanted her to leave. Jan handed Camille the can.

"God bless you," Camille said. "The people on the other side will appreciate this, I know."

"Do you know if anyone's still alive over there?" Jan asked.

"I think so, yes. We shall see. We've had reports."

From people or from angels? Jan wondered. She hoped the reports were from angels. She didn't want any tourists wandering over to this side of the mountain. They could be carrying something contagious.

There was no more to say. Still standing, Jan swallowed the dregs of her tea as Camille slipped on her sandals. As they went out the back door Camille asked, "You think the boats will get back before it gets dark?"

Jan laughed. "If they do they won't admit it to us. The men are looking forward to a binge, and this trip is their excuse. They're gone for two nights at least, Camille, and they'll come home hung over; you can count on it."

Camille's brow wrinkled. "You think so?" She had been secretly pleased when Ralph finished his last bottle of bourbon in June, although she'd pretended to mourn with him; he had seemed so depressed.

Camille's worried look made Jan laugh. "Hey, Camille, that's no way for God's chosen people to behave, is it? Like a bunch of drunks?"

"Where did they get the alcohol?" Camille asked. Bea had been asking if there was any up-country, because they were dry in town.

"Who knows, but mark my words, they'll be hung over when they get back."

"Oh my," said Camille.

"They're in God's hands, Camille."

"That's true. Well, I better be going."

Jan made a mistake as they passed by the generator under the porch. She kicked it.

"Oh, is that your wonderful generator?" Camille said. "I thought Michael was going to fix that."

"He just never gets around to it. Says we won't be able to get gasoline for it anyway."

"Oh, that's right. Where were you getting the fuel for it?"

"We'll get it going somehow," Jan said, avoiding the subject. No one knew, but she'd siphoned gasoline out of the gas pumps and stored it in containers in the shed. She'd stolen so much of it, making one trip after another from the station on the cliff. It was easy once the hoses where hooked up, but no one had seen her take it, no one knew where she'd hidden it, and if that was the way it stayed then she'd have fuel for a long time yet.

"Listen, Jan. Take it easy. You are pregnant and it's not so simple now, having that baby. Take care." Camille patted Jan's bulging abdomen, and then waved good-bye as she hurried down the path at the back of the house.

Alone again, Jan patted her own belly. Recently, the baby seemed to jump in her stomach every time Jan thought about it. She realized reluctantly that Camille was right; she did need more rest and, now that Camille had gone, she went into her room to lie down, burying herself in the comforter, trying to forget Camille's visit and the last can of pea soup.

In a dream she swayed over the stage, the rope twisted like a noose around her abdomen. She'd been swung down from the rafter on a rope pulley that was jerry-rigged over the stage for the high school play. She wished she was God rather than the angel. Could she be God in Camille's play? No, it was the angel who had all the lines. God never talked. But the rope wouldn't fit around her middle any more, not in this condition. Jan patted her stomach and shook her head. No angel. No god. Even though they didn't seem to know each other, she and Camille had known their parts in this play, and they played the duet perfectly. God made a world and God would swing down in the end, and there would be such applause and the play would end.

A white blast shook Jan out of her half sleep. It had only been a dream, but still her stomach contracted hard. Jan realized her teeth were clenched. Breathe deeply, she told herself, for the baby. After a few minutes the baby moved but Jan had fallen back to sleep.

The lights from the fires on the beach burned low and the men sat around complaining about their sunburns. In fact there hadn't been enough liquor to go around, not for the kind of night Ralph wanted, and not if they were going to have any left for the party once the boats returned. But, nevertheless, once the soldiers had left, the mood among the men had lightened. They enjoyed the comaraderie and passed around the few bottles they'd opened. A big pot of fish stew bubbled on the fire, and the men ate and ate, as if the pot didn't have a bottom. They'd thrown in most of the fish they caught, along with some vegetables. They'd even boiled a few lobsters and passed them around.

When the food was nearly gone and the bottles were empty, a silence came over the camp. Some of the men, including Koken, sat by the edge of the fire. Tomi sat between the fire and the tent, arranging the shells he had collected in a semi-circle around the tent entrance.

Michael wandered over by the water and sat by himself at the edge of the coral reef. He looked out over the water, thinking: Steven's out there now, Steven's reached the island. The scraggly boulders loomed up into the dark, black rock meeting black sky. Michael listened to the sound of the waves breaking on hard rocks. The beach was the birthplace of the island's old tales and fears. Now the fears tightened around Michael's stomach, at once repelling him and holding him. He was straining to hear the familiar sounds of planes making their last Kaane-Honolulu flight for the night, but, of course, there were no planes. The lights that flickered were not jets, only stars that were bright against the intense dark.

"Koken, do you think my dad's lonely there by himself?" Tomi asked shyly, affected by the darkness.

Koken was touched by the child's concern. "You go see?"

"It's too spooky over there."

Koken had always been afraid of the dark beach himself. He took Tomi's hand. "Let's go together," and the two crossed over the sand.

"Hey guy, how's it going, guy?" Koken called out. Michael startled, jumped up to his feet.

"The lobster's all gone, but there's more stew," Koken said, taking a seat on the rock.

Tomi sat down next to Michael and stared into the dark. Michael shot his eyes over the water.

"You think there's anyone out there?" Koken said. "I mean someone besides our guys in their boats?"

Michael shrugged.

"Michael, I been thinking. Maybe we could rig up something, just in case there are people over there on the other islands. I mean, who knows? Maybe this thing is isolated. Maybe it's okay on the mainland. How would we know?"

Michael's back straightened and he looked straight at Koken. "Maybe."

"And I was thinking," Koken continued, encouraged. "I got the mechanical sense and you know so much about the engineering. Maybe we could get some sort of radio and light system together, a kind of communication tower over here, and we could start signalling."

Koken had tried it before, and he knew the problems. But Michael had a better sense of how these things were done, and Koken wanted to try again. "I've checked out all the transistor chips, Michael. They're wrecked. Can't understand it, but they're no good for anything."

"Use old tubes," Michael said. Tomi smiled to hear his father's voice.

"Sure. Worth trying. The soldiers might be interested in working on it too. They might have some equipment..."

Michael's shoulders stiffened. "No, leave them out of it."

"Sure," Koken said. "But can I count on your help?"

Michael nodded. Koken could see him nod, yes, in the dark, and he put his arm around Tomi's shoulder. The boy's eyes had gone back and forth, studying the men's faces as they talked. He studied his father's face to see if he would say anything more. Maybe there would be more. Maybe some regular talk. It had been so long.

8

Update on demographics:

After exploring the area north of Kalawao the soldiers were able to confirm the death of all the residents in that area. The suspected cause of death is radiation poisoning. The area affected includes a small native-Hawaiian colony. I am a doctor, not a historian or priest. Other people will have to study the turn of events and impute meaning to the native people's demise. I simply record the data as one would submit an obituary, but let it be said that this doctor does not see meaning in the tragedy. It simply happened. It turned out thus. That is that.

As well, the resilience of the tourist population in the Kalawao area has been sorely tested and found wanting. They arrived for a holiday in the sun. It was not to be. Most must have been struck so deeply by grief, so far from their loved ones and the sources of their wealth, that they had no strength to resist infection after their relatively minor exposure to radiation.

A rescue operation on their behalf is being planned. The evangelical church up in Lono has organized a last-minute conversion expedition to the tourist areas. These hardy believers will deliver food and the word of God to the unfortunates in Kalawao who survived the radiation, the near starvation conditions, and the major epidemics which probably resulted from the poor sanitation in their quarters after April. I hope the members of the congregation don't catch anything. Undoubtedly the tourists will have their own brands of sores, infestations, and bacterial infections. My attempt to discourage the expedition has been futile, which leads me to the next topic.

The response of various religious groups to the war:

Historically and currently there are several religious group-ings on the island who have co-existed with a minimum of conflict. These groups responded to our crisis in very different ways. One group of Buddhists, those who live along the coast, just south of Ahupuaa, were hit hard, sustaining many early casualties, and have suffered a disproportionate number of deaths. Their religious observances are carried out with an austerity that led me at first to conclude that they had aban-doned their religious practices since April. However, in the late summer, at the time of the Bon Odari festival when they re-member their dead ancestors, the cemeteries and shrines were lit with candles and decorated with unusually delicate and artistic bouquets, lamps, and elaborate hand-painted banners. None of the customary dancing and feasting accompanied this manifestation, and we non-Buddhists were unaware that any organizing had been carried out. Yet, one evening the candles were lit, and by the end of the week many hillsides were alive with the flickering lights set beside the tiny shrines. The non-Buddhist residents, who traditionally participate in the Bon Odari as visitors, kept their distance—no flash cameras this year—and a hush settled down over the ancient festival. We observers did not enter into the reverence or mystery or what-ever it was that lined the faces of the Buddhists who are our neighbors. We stood aside.

Among the Christians, the mainline denominations have ceased their practices in the large churches. Perhaps congrega-ting in such large buildings, now that the tribe's numbers have been greatly reduced, brought home the reality of our situation with too sharp a clarity. It does tend to spoil one's taste for worship. Besides, several of the clergy died in the early days of the new times, and it has been rumored that the Catholic priest, a Franciscan, went into hiding up on Halepele. I have been informed that small groups do worship together in private homes.

On the other hand, the evangelical Christians faced up to the catastrophe with an irritating vigor and an exuberance that is shocking. They redoubled their evangelizing efforts and have even approached me, despite the fact that my stance against all organized religion has been public for some time. It is my firmly held opinion that anyone who believes in an afterlife, such as the one they are anticipating, simply hasn't spent enough time with dead bodies. By the time most people die they had just as well forget about their bodies, because they are shot to hell and rotting. These Christian enthusiasts' attitude infuriates people. The believers corner us to discuss points of faith, they parade in the streets, singing triumphantly, and then they redouble their efforts to evangelize we heathen.

Yet the vast majority on the island, haoles, Japanese, Chinese and Portuguese alike, maintain a secular stance. We have not sought refuge in myth or wild hopes of salvation. Subject occasionally to superstition perhaps, we still maintain our perspective. We continue to persist.

Report on food production:

The women's taro project is progressing, and after the first few brushes with failure the women are witnessing growth in the plants and the successful operation of the irrigation systems. The women are now planning to move on to cultivating rice, which has been grown successfully on the island for centuries, but not in sufficient volume to fill the island's needs today. And now, even though I am a doctor, a good doctor and one of the few still practising the art, now they expect me to hoe and to weed. Okay, I do it.

Our sources of protein will eventually be supplemented by the animals that will be brought back from Pua Island. However, goat and mutton will be feast foods, not regular supplements to the diet, until the flocks are firmly established.

A Letter:

Marilyn Nakatsura had the habit of writing to her great-aunt in Japan on the first Monday of every month. Late last April, when the soldiers had proclaimed that it was safe to come out of our houses, Marilyn hurried to catch up on her correspondence and mailed the following letter. Several weeks later, in a fit of rage, upon realizing that everything was not going to return to normal in the immediate future, she knocked over the mail box, emptied it and retrieved the letter. Last week she gave it to me as a document of those early weeks in the new times.

Dear Auntie,   *April 29*
How are you? I am so afraid for you. Not knowing. I will trust you are fine. Did you hear of our predicament? Well, rest assured, your family here is fine. Mommy and Dad are fine. Omatsu and I had to stay in our home for two weeks. They were dreadful times. Not knowing. That is why I did not write to you earlier. We were hiding, but as soon as the officials signalled that it was safe to come out, I drove way up past Lono to check on Mom and Dad. I was so terribly <u>frightened</u>. On top of everything else, there had been a bomb or something that exploded up that way. But no worry. They are <u>fine</u> and I wanted to write to you right away to tell you so. We are worried, that is all. There has been such talk. And we have heard nothing from off the island.

There is such talk as you would not believe. Talk of people dying, talk of missiles and earthquakes and complete annihilation. I believe people are jumping to conclusions. There has been so little evidence that something so awful has happened. That is another reason I am writing to you. Please, Auntie, I know you are not much of a reader, but please collect everything you can find about this in the newspapers and send them to Omatsu and me <u>right away</u>. It would be very reassuring to know something more about this. We have gotten no news. So please hurry.

You are my beloved Aunt. I wish you were with us now. At this time, when my baby is growing inside me so strong, I wish you were here so I could share all this with you. I think that I have felt life inside. It is so hard to tell. There is a woman here, Teruko Masaoka. You would like her. She used to be a midwife, or perhaps it was her mother who was a midwife in

Japan, and she knows a great deal. She told me that it is very early to feel life, if that is what I was feeling, and that it is good luck for the baby. Have you ever heard this? I am so <u>happy</u> about the baby. So is Omatsu. He tells me not to worry, to hope for the best and everything will be all right. I do believe him. That everything will be fine. Oma is such a good man. Some people tease me, say he is as ugly as a blowfish, but he is <u>beautiful</u> to me.

And he sees things the way I do. There are people here that mope about and say things like "Why go on?" and "Why has this happened?" as if they know for sure what has happened. They do not know. And their prattling on like that sounds to me like stupid children that ask "Why? Why? Why?" all the time just to bother their parents. They delight in the sounds of their own voices, no matter if it disturbs other people. I am sorry to say this, but I really hate people like that.

I must go now, but wanted you not to worry so I wrote to you right away. There is an awful smell that makes me feel ill. Oma says it is my imagination. Other than that, I have no more morning sickness. We are <u>happy</u> and strong and will be fine. Please do send me those newspapers, and please <u>don't</u> worry.

> *With my love,*
> *Marilyn*

9

Steven was standing up front on the first outrigger that returned the next day, his belly swollen with the meat he had gulped down through the night. The boats were loaded with the cages now containing sheep and goats, and the ruckus could be heard across the water. Steven shouted and waved his spear to the men and young boys on the beach, who waded into the water to help haul the outriggers onto the sand. An older boy on the outrigger threw a sheepskin on Steven's back and tossed him onto the sand bar. Steven grinned and punched both his fists up over his head into the air.

One slaughtered sheep was carried up on the beach, hoofs tied to a pole. The men on shore had built a frame around the fire, and the pole was propped up at each end of the frame, so the meat hung over the fire that had burnt down to coals. Now more logs were thrown on top of the coals, the older men tending to the fire, careful that the flames didn't lick the meat. Drinks were poured. Sushi, fruit, nuts and vegetables that had been stashed in men's packs materialized and were passed around, but what everyone wanted, what made them huddle near the fire on the hot beach, was the meat. Bits of cooked meat that the young men had brought back from Pua Island, having butchered, sliced, and barbecued it on the island the night before, were also passed around and grease soon covered everyone's hands and mouths. The partying had begun in earnest.

Two days later Jan came out of the kitchen to see Steven in the doorway, a dark shape lit from behind by the sun.

"Hi, Steven," she called to him and laughed. He was wearing only his underpants with a sheepskin draped over his back. But Steven didn't laugh. He leaned his spear against the door jamb and walked toward her.

"It went okay," he said and, before Jan could say more, he pulled out the large slab of meat that was hidden behind his back. He walked past her and flung the meat onto the kitchen counter.

That day Michael began working on the drawings for a search

light that could send a beam in a semicircle across the water, and a radio to send continuous SOS signals, both powered by a single DC source. For several days he kept up the work, hunched over the drawings, perfecting and simplifying the designs, consulting with Koken and adjusting them if Koken told him a particular part would be hard to find. The Ito's living room was soon strewn with papers.

Jan looked over Michael's shoulder, asking him what he was doing. He grunted short answers to her questions. The dizzying maze of pencil lines didn't mean a thing to her.

Finally it was Koken, when he came up the mountain to show Michael some radio tubes he'd found, who explained what they were trying to build. At first Jan was enthusiastic. "So you really think it might work?" she asked, peering down at the drawings. Then she sighed. "Yeah, it might work. Or maybe it will work, and then not work..."

Koken shook his head at Jan, warning her not to say anything more. Jan pushed her hair off her forehead and turned away. Okay, she thought, if there's someone out there why hasn't anyone contacted us? Not knowing seemed to Jan to be a kind of knowing.

"How the hell are you going to find time to build all this?" she asked, sweeping her hand across the drawings.

Both men looked up from the drawings and Koken grinned. "He's got the brains and I've got the brawn."

Koken looked old now, Jan realized as she slumped onto the couch watching the men draw and erase lines, making up the list of screws, wires, tubes and lumber they needed. He had never looked so old to her before. They'd been friends over the years; he and Teri were almost like parents to Mike and Jan. When Koken got up to leave he smiled over at Jan, trying to get her attention, but she did not respond. He winked at Michael as he picked up the list. "No problem for me. I'll have this stuff by next week," he said as he left, lumbering out through the front door.

"So you talk to Koken," she said to Michael when she was sure Koken was out of ear shot. "It's just me that's frozen out." Michael continued rolling up the papers.

"It's kind of funny, you building a communications tower when you don't have anything to say to your own wife." Still Michael didn't respond. She shouted, "Well, why won't you talk with me?"

Michael said nothing.

"Talk, damn it. Why not talk with me?"

Michael sneered, "You never have anything to say."

Jan turned on her heels and stomped into the kitchen.

A moment later he came up behind her and put a hand on her shoulder. Her body stiffened under his touch, but he came around, standing in front of her, and stared into her eyes. She didn't blink, nor did he. Then her face finally relaxed. He continued staring, but the corners of his mouth rose, just a little, and he let go, picked up the roll of drawings and went out.

Michael didn't return that night and Jan slept fitfully. When she awoke the next day it was late in the morning, and remnants of dreams still clung to her. She was supposed to join the other women in the taro paddies, but she just couldn't get herself out of bed. She called the boys and told them to get their things together.

"Do we have to go, Mom?" Tomi sulked.

Steven looked over Tomi's shoulder at her, through the bedroom doorway. He was holding his spear and said nothing.

"Let me get up and get some breakfast and then we'll go. Grab something for yourselves to eat," she said, propping herself up on her elbows.

"No Mommy, I'm tired. I'm too tired to go that far away," Tomi whined.

"It's not that far," Jan said, but she herself fell back onto her pillow. She felt a dead weight pressing down on her chest. It was too far, she thought.

When she finally managed to lift herself out of bed, she noticed how her belly sagged. She leaned against the side table, then pulled up her shoulders and breathed in. Her skin became hot as she stretched. She walked into the kitchen, and realized she wasn't hungry. Throwing some fruit and nuts into a bag, she called the boys and headed out the door. Half the morning was gone already and nothing to show for it.

Bea had arrived early at the taro paddies that morning, wearing a raw silk pant suit, that was now spotted with mud and frayed around the cuffs. Still, Camille's eyebrows rose when they met on the path. "Wow, Dr. Bea. That's a nice outfit. But you shouldn't work in that. You'll muss it up."

"No problem. My work clothes are in shreds so I thought I'd start on these. I certainly don't need them anymore for the office." She looked at Camille. "I thought you'd be gone by now."

"We're leaving tomorrow. Don't spoil that nice suit, Dr. Bea. Take it easy today."

"No problem," Bea said. Sitting down against the retaining wall, she pulled out one of her notebooks and began jotting something down just as she saw Teri coming up on the path.

Teri winced at the sight of Bea, and turned her head away. She didn't want to meet Bea's eyes now.

Bea looked up and saw Teri's expression. "What happened?"

Teri hesitated before she spoke, kicking up the dirt with her toe. "Marilyn was losing the baby, and losing blood. I tried everything. I massaged her uterus, I had her husband try to get you. Koken and Michael were down there too. They ran like madmen, trying to find you, but you weren't anywhere to be found."

But Bea had seen it all before, had anticipated this. "There was nothing I could have done that you didn't do," she said.

"I know," Teri's mumbled. "There was nothing anyone could have done."

"Still, I'm sorry I wasn't there to help you," Bea said, looking away from Teri. "I'll tell the others."

Bea shuffled over toward the lower paddies, where the group of women were working. Teri stayed behind. She didn't want to talk, and if they turned to her, expecting her to comfort them, it would be too much for her. She stood watching the ants on the path move dirt and food along.

When they heard about Marilyn, the women stiffened. Camille was immediately afraid for Jan and wanted answers from Bea. "How many does that leave? Maybe only four or five women carrying babies on the whole island, and nobody's become pregnant. You're the doctor. Tell us what's happening."

Bea had no energy left for these questions. "I thought you were leaving, Camille. Why don't you go. See how many you can save."

After some time Teri wandered down toward the paddies herself. Taking up a shovel, she joined the women as they started to repair the wall on the lower terrace.

Jan's walk down the mountain made her feel stronger. Plumeria bloomed along the road, and she filled her pockets with the nuts from a small tree of ripe litchi. The boys followed behind with their slingshots, looking for birds to aim at. When Jan arrived at the taro paddies the women looked up from their work. For an instant they looked like skeletons to Jan, their deep-set eyes hollow. She caught her breath as she stared back.

"Sorry I'm late," she stammered. "Hey, what's the matter here?"

Camille spoke first. "We've been at it for awhile. Just getting tired."

"That's why I hurried. I didn't want to miss lunch break," Jan laughed.

"And it's just about that time," Bea said, standing up and stretching, smiling weakly at Jan.

"Hey, I really am sorry I'm so late. I just couldn't get going," Jan said.

"Tomi," Teri said. "Go call the little ones. Tell them it's lunch." Tomi took off, calling to the other children, who ran in from the woods at the first mention of food, tumbling over each other. The women gathered into a tight knot, all of them looking over at Bea. She was silently appointed to tell Jan about Marilyn's death.

There was no sense being casual. These were Jan's friends, and Bea looked over her shoulder to see if anyone would come forward now to help. No, she'd been appointed because she was the doctor. She put her arm over Jan's shoulder, to take her aside, and for once Jan didn't shrug it off. "Come here a minute, Jan. We need to talk about something."

Jan did not seem so interested in the myriad of facts that Bea presented her with, only one fact: Marilyn had died from loss of blood, and without blood transfusions no one could do anything about it. When Bea had finished, she looked right in Jan's eyes. Bea was surprised. Jan looked sympathetic, not afraid.

"There's nothing you can do?" Jan asked.

"In a case like that now? Nothing."

"It must be hell."

"I didn't even get there last night."

"I'll probably be on my own too."

"Perhaps."

"Okay."

The women glanced over furtively, afraid to see Jan's expression. They wanted to chatter for Jan's sake, to dissipate fear, to fill in silences, but when Bea and Jan joined the group there was nothing to say. They ate and Teri slid over to sit next to Jan.

"Michael was at our house last night, when I was called over to help Marilyn. He and Koken came with me. He tried to help with Marilyn; he did everything he could. That's why he didn't make it home." Teri put her hand on Jan's knee.

"That's okay," Jan said. "I wasn't worried."

"He said he'd meet you and the boys at the house tonight."

"Yeah, that's what I told the kids."

10

After the food was passed around, Steven led the little children up to the higher paddy to eat their lunch, the very youngest scampering at the end of the line, trying to keep up. Suddenly, reaching the top and climbing up onto the retaining wall, the children's eyes fixed on what they saw in the paddy, and several children started screaming. The women, hearing their shouts, raced up the hill after them. Camille was the first to reach the children in the upper paddy and, looking into the pool of water, she shooed the children away. Putting her hand out to keep the other women from approaching, she moved back down to join the group herself.

"It's nothing, kids. He's just taking a bath," she said to the children. Her face was pale. "Now leave him alone. He doesn't want you bothering him. Go back to the woods where you were playing before." The kids looked at her, confused, but they did what they were told, running off into the woods to finish their meal there. Only Steven and Tomi stayed in the lower paddy, Tomi huddled next to Jan, pressing against her legs. Jan's hands clutched Tomi's small shoulders to reassure him.

"It's a soldier," Camille told the women. "He looks quite dead. I think he's been shot."

Tomi stuttered quietly, "Mommy, Mommy. What is wrong with him, Mommy? How come he's dead?"

"He was shot, stupid," Steven muttered.

Suddenly Jan's body wrenched with a pain, an aching exhaustion she knew no amount of sleep would overcome. She leaned on Tomi's shoulders now for support. She looked down at her two sons. All that had happened since April merged into this sensation of utter fatigue.

"Mommy? Are you okay?" Tomi asked.

"Steven, take Tomi. Go with the other children," she whispered, trying to hold herself up, letting go of Tomi.

"Oh, Mom," Steven whined, but he nudged his brother and the

two of them wandered a short distance away. But instead of heading into the woods, they crept up the hill at the edge of the paddies. They moved slowly until they had reached the top of the slope, above the upper paddy. At the edge of the paddy the two boys peered down at the soldier's body.

Jan remained in the lower paddy while the other women climbed up the hill, now seemingly concerned only with the disposal of the body. Jan's questions weren't their questions. They moved efficiently. Was there no pain if you didn't know the dead? Jan wondered. Did the soldier's body represent just another task, disposal for the sake of sanitation? It was certainly not burdened with sentiment, or with what could have been, or with what was hoped for.

The women disposed of the body by dragging it across the upper paddy toward the underbrush. There was a ditch they'd dug in that area when they had built the retaining walls. It had been meant for compost, but now it would be a grave.

Somewhere this man will be missed, Jan thought. He looked about thirty. Is there nothing left for unknown dead people—not even grief? It's fine for a soldier to die, a relief to these women who didn't trust him; is that what they feel, or maybe they feel only indifference? The dead feel nothing. What is this sentimentality? Not even Teri is reacting with horror. Teri seems to feel nothing. And Tomi isn't afraid anymore. Look at him up there. He seems more curious than upset by the murder. Steven, standing on top of the retaining wall, his spear stuck in the ground, looks like a victor who's taken the hill.

Jan, looking up at Steven, shuddered and then remembered; the soldier had been shot, not speared. She stood motionless. Realizing this man had been murdered, she felt alone. This is different from the other kind of dying; this is something to be remarked upon, she thought. This man was killed deliberately, here. Perhaps we know the killer. Perhaps it is one of us.

Jan stared at Camille. Would she baptize the soldier post-humously? Would she pray for him? Apparently not. Camille's wraith-like frame pulled against the dead weight, as she helped the other women drag the body across the paddy. Will prayers come later? But Camille showed no signs of religious fervor. She merely helped complete the task. The job was disgusting; the water had bloated the corpse. Yet, the women had seen so much dying, they knew the nausea passed quickly.

Jan's hands quivered and she held them hard against her sides. Weren't all the deaths since April murder? Someone on each side had aimed missiles, had calculated the casualties in advance. Had they counted themselves in? Had they counted their families in before filing their notes and going home for supper? Why horror over one soldier? Because I saw this man's face? Death with a face—it's all the same to the dead man, she thought. Death isn't compounded because it's lost its anonymity. Involuntarily Jan shook her head. No, this was murder, this was a different dying.

The women threw some dirt into the ditch to cover the body. At first the dirt just dusted the soldier's whole shape, sticking to his wet skin and clothes until he looked like a mummy. Then, as the dirt piled up, the shape of the body blurred. Two women stayed behind to continue filling in the ditch while the others returned to work. Tomi and Steven went back into the woods to join the other children and finish their food.

Jan slipped away unnoticed from the taro paddy to the end of the path. She felt shivers of nausea throughout her whole body. At the end of the path she found an exposed rock and sat down to get her breath. The sun was warm on her face and arms. The shivering was subsiding. From that vantage point the island was spread out at her feet. The rain she could see falling over by the Pali had brought out a rainbow. The landscape looked unaffected, as if nothing had happened on the island in the last year, the last century. The greens faded to brown and pale tan by the beaches. Blue ocean met blue sky.

The woods were so near the path that, from where she was sitting, Jan could hear the children playing. It was a familiar sound, comforting to her. Leaning back against the rock she massaged her belly to calm herself. It's perfect, she thought. A beautiful mound. An ivory tower belly. Smooth like the whale.

The sound of the children playing wound its way through her thoughts. She sat quietly, thinking about the new baby. The dead soldier seemed far away now. Bea's words slipped away from her.

Jan wanted a girl this time, a girl who would play paper dolls with her. She remembered playing paper dolls with her sister. One day the dolls would be models, strutting here and there; oh how elegant; little papers with tabs would become gowns and veils and purses; empty spools of thread were thrones and tables; the spools became stools for the circus elephants; more paper dresses, clown costumes and leotards with tutu skirts. Jan's doll was the best trapeze artist, flying through the air until the perfect man, the man like Daddy, would catch her just before she was to plunge to the ground. Back and forth they'd swing; careful now.

The baby turned over. Jan could see the movement on her belly and she giggled, massaging the lump, bringing her hands over her belly button, then around the sides just as a birth instructor had taught her during her first pregnancy. She had stared at her changing body with amazement mixed with horror the first time. The changes seemed so irreversible. The flat stomach had bloated up like a drowned mammal washed up on shore.

The changes had disgusted Jan, until the baby inside was big enough that when it—little anonymous Steven—turned over, she could see the ripple. Jan patted her belly. It had been so much easier the second time around; she had trusted her body by then. She could have delivered Tomi herself. She was in control. She was a plant in full bloom with huge red blossoms, and Tomi was born underneath, peeking out from beneath the blossoms and green foliage.

During each pregnancy Jan had felt as if part of her body was ripening as it expanded, and oddly, even amidst all the recent deaths, she'd found herself still feeling in control of her own body, her life reduced to its most essential concerns, food, touch, sleep, skin, the baby growing within her. For food, she and the other women had begun to make the earth take on new shapes, and as the plants grew up around their ankles, so the women seemed to grow. They were banding together to manage the essentials, and there was satisfaction and rest at the end of the day. Despite the disasters, her body felt alive. Only the soldier's murder had seemed to threaten that life.

The sound of the children playing up the hill grew louder. She climbed a little way up the hill so she could watch their games.

"Bang, bang, you're dead," Jan heard Tomi scream.

"I am not. You are dead. Bang bang bang," another child yelled at him.

Jan's anger turned to rage as she stood up by the rock and saw the children pointing their sticks at each other. "Stop playing that!" she shouted at them. Her voice carried. They looked up at her, surprised.

The noise subsided. "Ah, Ma," Steven grumbled up to her.

"I mean it," Jan bellowed.

"Okay." Steven turned to his brother. "Tomi, you be trail guide and we'll go hunting for the haul that the soldiers left on the mountain." The boys crouched over and began scaling their way down the path, further away from Jan, toward the woods.

"Hey, Robert, stay behind me. You want to get hit by the spear?" Steven ordered, as they moved away up the hill.

Jan tried to settle back down onto the ground, but she was trembling again. She massaged her abdomen, whispering to the baby within, "There you go. You're doing fine. It's marvelous you've happened at all...Shh," she whispered.

Jan's skin began to feel warm, as she remembered Michael touching her. After years together they knew each other's favorite spots. Michael had been so excited about having another baby they'd made love every night for weeks. It was special sex, baby-making sex. It was so hopeful. "Get the baby off to the right start," Michael had teased. "Rock the baby, rock the baby," and he had rocked Jan, rubbing her body. Then turning over, they'd have sex again. And again. Jan felt her face redden now in the paddy, remembering those nights. One evening was all it took, maybe twenty minutes, for a whole new life to begin. When had it happened? Pray God, she thought, it was one of those nights in March, not a terrified night in April when we were hiding in the house, clutching at each other, the boys having finally fallen asleep.

"*Brrrrrrrroom. CRASH!*" The sound of the boys' imagined bomb blew up in Jan's imagination. A war. A holocaust. Nothing.

Jan shrieked and jumped to her feet. She stared down the hill. Only one child was standing, sheepishly, his hands held out from his sides. The others lay face down, pretending to be dead. Staring down at them, Jan felt her stomach pull tight. She gagged and threw up. Then everything went blank.

Somehow, she realized in the grey haze that surrounded her as she came round, the women had managed to carry her up the mountain to her house. She knew she was lying on the floor of her own living room. She recognized the stained glass window, the faces oddly foreshortened at this angle. She lay in a pool of warm liquid. Michael held her. His face was wet with perspiration and tears. He was rubbing her belly and muttering over again and again, "My baby, my baby."

As she came around, she looked at him quizically. "Are you all right, honey?" she asked.

His face lit up and his voice rose slightly, "My baby."

"Your baby? What about me?" Jan laughed. She put her hand on the floor and felt the moisture. "Hey, Michael, we're sitting in a swamp. Sorry about all this," and she looked at her hand. Expecting vomit, she was shaken to see that there was a pool of blood dripping from under her sun dress, the warm liquid sticking to her inner thighs. "What the hell? Hey, I'm bleeding!"

Michael wouldn't let her stand up. "No, Jan. Stay. Dr. Bea says be still. Don't move."

Jan saw Dr. Bea peering over Michael's shoulder. She was saying something, but Jan could not make out the words. The dizziness returned, but Michael's voice urged Jan to stay awake.

"Michael, you can talk," she muttered. The sarcasm stung him. Immediately Jan regretted having said it. Why can't I be civil? she wondered. I could just shut up. But then Jan no longer knew if she was speaking aloud or to herself. Slumping back into his arms she told Michael that she knew this baby was going to be a girl. She babbled on about the dead soldier, about not having felt well all day. Then she remembered that Marilyn had died and she clung to Michael, but she didn't want to talk about that. Instead she withdrew, travelling deep inside her body. No, she wasn't going to die. She wasn't going to lose the baby. The life inside was strong. She passed in and out of consciousness. She dreamt that God was carrying her, urging her to hold on, to take care of the child. The god-midwife coaxed her onto a bed of plants, whispering, "The child wants to be born. Be strong. Heal." There was food growing all around, with red flowers and bedding of soft matted grass.

Jan dragged herself forward, back into consciousness. Michael was still holding her, trembling, crying.

"Shh, I'm going to be fine," she reassured him. Her voice sounded weak in her own ears. "I had a dream about the baby, Michael. It's very special. Something to do with God's promise."

"It's okay. Just be still." He sounded almost strong.

Jan knew he thought she was crazy or dying. She became determined to pull herself back to him. "I'm sorry about all this slush, Michael." She felt the moisture on his shirt as he held her.

"It's no problem."

"Oh, of course not," she smiled at him. Then the dizziness overcame her.

At the foot of the mountain, in their barracks in Mahele, the thirteen remaining soldiers ate their dinner of rice and fruit together, waiting for their buddy to come back. Talk was short; the guy had been missing for more than a day. He was the oldest of them, at thirty-two years old, and had been something of a leader for the group ever since the sergeant had been blown up. It would have been bad luck to count him among their dead, so they waited.

Jack was looking out the window. "From now on I think we should travel in pairs," he said into the silence and turned around to face the guy sitting down at the desk. "You want to play gin?" he asked.

The soldier pulled a deck of cards out from the desk drawer, and Jack pulled up a chair.

"Remember that night in boot camp?" Jack asked as he shuffled the deck. "Remember when we first got news we'd be stationed in Hawaii? I thought it was a gift from the army."

As the game began, Jack thought back. They'd all packed up. The unmarried men bought skimpy swim trunks; the married guys told their families it wouldn't be long before they'd get settled in and could bring them over. Married housing was scarce. That was the big hold-up. Jack had explained this to his wife. He remembered his first few months in Honolulu. He had bought a car so he could look for an apartment that he and his wife could afford. It would take her some time to find a job, he figured, so the place had to be cheap. Now, when he couldn't help but think about it, it made him sick. Why had he waited? Why didn't she come with him at the start?

During those first weeks he and his buddies had driven all around the island. A few of the guys dated rich women on holiday in Honolulu. Cruising the beaches, checking out the tourist sights and the bars, took all their off-duty time. That was when they were on Oahu.

That was a year ago. Now they clung to each other. They hadn't thought of women in months. They clung to their silence and their civil defence manual. Occasionally one of them would step forward, take charge and make plans. But nothing ever came of it, or worse: more soldiers would get sick, die, or just disappear.

"You know what really makes my skin crawl around here?" Jack's partner said, dealing out another hand. "Not these folks making fun of us. I mean, its no wonder they aren't crazy about the army now."

"Yeah," Jack nodded, but in fact the locals stung and infuriated him. He couldn't be blamed for this. He hadn't bombed anything.

Jack's partner continued. "It's just that these Japs...there are so many of them. There are more of them here than there were in San Francisco, and they seemed to be everywhere in San Francisco."

"You better not let them hear you call them Japs."

"Hell no. You think I'm crazy?"

"No."

"It's just there's so many of these stonefaced Japs," the soldier muttered, lowering his voice. "And they really are stonefaced. You notice that?"

"Yeah," Jack said.

At midnight Jack and his partner put away the cards, turned out the lantern and went to bed. Their buddy still hadn't come back.

11

October 13

"Oblivion: n. Fame's eternal dumping ground. Cold storage
for high hopes. A dormitory without an alarm clock."
Ambrose Bierce's *The Devil's Dictionary*.

An update on livestock experiments:
Rabbit-raising continues, despite the death of the original
couple. Camille had the first rabbit pair, Marigold and Marshmallow, and she promised Ralph she would serve their off-
spring for dinner, or trade them with neighbors, if he promised
not to harm the original pets. He promised, and the rabbits
hopped about their hutch in relative safety until, after parenting
two litters, both parents died. Now Camille's youngest son has
a new set of slippers; left Marigold, right Marshmallow. Several
breeding pairs were taken from the two litters and were adopted
by two other families up in Lono. Those rabbits are doing
well.
The sheep and goats from Pua Island have adapted to
Kaane. The entire flock is still alive, save one sheep that disappeared. The soldiers were accused of stealing it, although there
was no evidence indicating that they were even in the area at the
time.

Population study:
1) The soldier population is decreasing. I have been asked
to investigate the recent soldiers' disappearances, three having
disappeared in the last two weeks. Their spokesman approached me and I, of course, refused to aid them in their
investigation. I have problems of my own, after all. However, I
did inform him that a soldier was found dead from a bullet

wound in the taro paddy and, since no gun was found in the area, suicide had been ruled out. The spokesman took this news badly, so badly that, upon observing his reaction, I also ruled out the possibility that the dead man had been shot by one of his comrades in a dispute. The soldier's face fell into his hands; he didn't want me to see him snivelling. After a while, wiping his nose on his sleeve, he told me that our lack of concern for their welfare, considering our own circumstances, was understandable and that he would not hold it against us. That was decent of him. I told him so.

2) The incidence of maternal death is increasing. Marilyn Nakatsura's death resulted from internal hemorrhage following a spontaneous abortion in the third trimester of her pregnancy. Marilyn could have survived either the miscarriage or an abortion had she been given proper medical care, but neither the medical supplies nor the instrumentation necessary for good care were available. The fetus, mind you, could not have been saved under any circumstances. Teri Masaoka reported to me, having examined it, that it was severly malformed.

It appears, then, that the information and directions given in the soldiers' manual were correct after all; first term abortions should have been encouraged, although the suggestion was resisted by the women involved and, in fact, proper facilities weren't really available in any case. But here is the dilemma we face now: it is too late to perform abortions on those women who are still pregnant, even though the fetuses are almost certainly not viable, without endangering the mother's life. Therefore we are committed to going full-term with those pregnant women who received massive doses of radiation in their first trimester. We try to be cheerful and evasive about the fact that they are almost certainly mothering little monsters, but it is not easy to keep the facts from them altogether.

October 28

Report on the Evangelicals' Mission to the Tourist Area:

The congregation from the Church of Jesus returned from their expedition last week. They reported that the tourist population is now down to a handful of small bands surviving on what they can scavenge.

The faith of these true believers is finally shaken. In the tourist area they encountered people who have abandoned any pretence of civilization. Crazed with hunger and disease, the tourists are now scavengers, scampering from one feast of fruit to their next, their stomachs distended, their eyes glazed with fever. In short, they were not receptive to the word of God.

Nor were the food supplies the congregation brought of much use in the absence of the most rudimentary elements of civilization. The tourists had no can opener to open the canned goods they were offered, no fire to boil water, no pans or utensils, and they were so afraid that ghosts were lurking about in the hotels they refused to go back and fetch basic cooking utensils from the hotel kitchens. And, while the congregation had precious little to give the tourists, they received much: hepatitis, lice, and some extremely contagious diseases that I am simply not able to diagnose. Several members of the congregation died from this illness on the return trip, as did fifteen of the twenty-three tourists who returned with the congregation.

So the expedition was not the purifying experience that the congregation had anticipated. Their eyelids twitch when they tell their stories. They describe people hardly recognizable as human, people with torn clothes hanging like dead leaves on sun-scorched limbs, sores oozing on the bodies of people too depraved to notice. There are descriptions of people consumed by a pain centered in their bellies, bellies bloated from malnutrition or parasites. And as members of the congregation describe these people, they themselves double over, clasping their own bellies. Their hope of inspiring one last mass conversion to Christ was transformed and distorted into a realized hell. Their mission ended before it had begun. In the end, members of the congregation pounded the tops off cans and ate the food that was to be the converts' prize.

After encountering the skeletal forms of those who were to

have been the final converts, finally it occurred to these Christians that this catastrophe we've lived since April is, in some ways, something other than a religious drama. Remarkable. When we buried the first victims did they feel smug, counting those lives as cannon fodder in a holy war? But I digress.

The congregation listened to the surviving tourists tell stories of mass graves that had been dug after fever and some intestinal disease raged through the tourist population. Ironically, such epidemics are not new on the island. Four hundred years ago similar epidemics decimated the indigenous population. Now it is claiming the invaders, the local workers, and the unlucky tourists as well. The few tourists who survived the first wave of epidemic have lived out their days like scavenging animals.

It wasn't long before it dawned on the congregation, most of them anyway, that they had made a terrible mistake. (The reverend remains unconvinced to this day.) They quickly gathered up their things, intending to head back across the island immediately, but they needed fresh water and a few supplies. Some of the tourist nomads begged to be brought back here and, as a gesture of good will, showed the congregation their water source. Perhaps giving in to a taste for nostalgia, the believers baptized the tourists in the water and filled their jugs, preparing to begin the hike back at once. However many of the children on the expedition then became deathly ill, vomiting, covered with rashes, and hardly able to breathe. The group was forced to camp by the water supply for about a week before giving the little ones back to the earth.

Camille Evans' daughter, Susan, was among the casualties. Camille has since stopped speaking altogether.

When the group finally did return, we doctors suspected that the tourists had exposed them to cholera, but we cannot be certain. The residents in Mahele who initially went to welcome the congregation froze in their tracks when they saw the ragged, sickly bunch. Fear turned to fury. Rumors spread like fire. A riot nearly ensued. The doctors intervened, and arrangements for quarantining the congregation in the old athletic facility were hastily completed.

The people down-country, living around Mahele, have threatened to shoot anyone in the congregation who ventures out of the quarantine area. The quarantine in the old athletic facility was itself a compromise. The townspeople were furious and frightened as they recognized the dirty, yellow-eyed congregation and realized that they were being exposed to still more dangerous diseases. Isolation was considered a moderate proposal, a demand for immediate execution being the more extreme response.

Reverend Thompson turned his congregation over to me and I have been caring for them, remaining in isolation myself. The other doctors in Mahele are critical of my decision to accept responsibility for these adventurers. I suspect the doctors' critique is not without substance—I am not even sure of my motives—but to see their broken faith reminds me of something very old, almost forgotten, that I want to own and polish as I would an antique.

Whatever it was that they sought among the tourists, that which would buttress their faith, they did not find it. Instead, the death of their own members before Jesus' return broke their hearts and bodies. Now these people are dislocated and disoriented. And perhaps that is what compelled me to stay here in the facility with them, to keep company with people who, like me, have lost. They tolerate my bitter complaining about the absence of tobacco and they share the details of their myth and their hopes with me, offering me pieces of this sign and that for consolation. But faith doesn't dance in their eyes, eyes that now see only Kaane, a decimated little island of common people, rather than the kingdom that was to come.

A wise man, Mr. Wittingham, makes his rounds among the cots. "We were wrong again!" he announces. A chuckle can be detected in his voice. "It wasn't the time. What a lot of fools we are! Signs, signs! St. Paul must be laughing. More than once he picked up the broken pieces of those who pointed to signs, signs! It is in the waiting. That is God's love—waiting, waiting..."

Mr. Wittingham really bothers the reverend with this talk.

In consideration of their condition I recommend a softer bed-side manner myself. They are dying, after all; why rub their noses in it?

So I am residing in an athletic facility. Cots and food have been delivered. My main effort is to provide the patients with nourishment, in the hope that improved nutrition (and any food is improvement) will halt the spread of disease and prevent more fatalities. Those clearly infected are kept in a separate area within the facility. I suspect that none of the tourists who came here have much chance of surviving, they are so badly run down. Their resistance is quite low and, with no immunities built up prior to the new time, their trim, tanned bodies were easy prey for this infection.

I am making systematic notes now on the progression of the various afflictions and their treatments. The main focus is on what might be a cholera outbreak. Exposure to radiation seems to have suppressed the entire population's immunities and I am concerned that this outbreak could easily spread beyond this compound. We can do no more than we are doing, but I intend to produce charts and graphs for my colleagues to dwell on. That will please them; they will think it was noble for me to have agreed to remain in the facility. I am a doctor, after all, with a particular penchant for research.

By next week I will have trained the people here to carry on and provide the necessary nursing care for their own. If I haven't contracted any disease myself by then I will leave, isolate myself in my home for two weeks to be certain no one else is exposed, and then count my gains and losses.

12

Second report on conditions in the facility, upon leaving the facility:

I left the athletic facility today knowing that my services were no longer of value. My regular patients, in my absence, are without medical care and they need my attention. I am particularly anxious to look in on my one remaining pregnant patient, Jan Ito, who I left several weeks ago in serious but stable condition under Teri Masaoka's care, in order to attend to the congregation. Teri, I suppose, is as capable as anyone on Kaane to handle such a case, but I want to see the patient myself. The fetal development has been remarkably normal throughout this pregnancy.

The other reason I left the athletic facility was concern for my personal safety, and for my health, as conditions began to further deteriorate. Let me explain: those confined to the facility are of two general types; while one group is quite docile, the other group is experiencing a crisis of faith that has rendered them both hostile and explosive. Where they once awaited their bodily transportation to Israel to witness the second coming, they now doubt the reverend's predictions of the imminent millenium and they have ceased their vigil.

They feel duped. Humiliated, hungry, and yet still clear-thinking enough to recognize that their hunger is making them more susceptible to contagious disease, they are making plans to leave the facility regardless of the danger to themselves and those in the town. Since the residents of Mahele have threatened to kill anyone who leaves the athletic facility, the group may be forced into the hills, either in the Pali Beach area or up on the mountain, to survive as best they can by scavenging.

Their loss of faith has resulted in an overall gain in their personal commitment to survive.

For their part, the residents in Mahele have not lived up to their promise to provide those in quarantine with adequate food and water. Everyone in the facility is bitter about that, despite my attempts to offer a more balanced perspective. The town is rightfully angry; after all, the congregation endangered their lives by exposing them to still more disease. Furthermore, the food people leave for those quarantined in the facility is food they might soon need themselves, since the supply is tenuous, at least until crop diversification can be achieved and that may take another year.

Then there is the perennial problem of a limited capacity for compassion. The residents in Mahele cannot possibly imagine the suffering those in the facility have experienced. To vomit again and again until your eyes sink into your head from dehydration, with no tea to soothe your throat, no thin soup, not even water; the pain wrenches their bony frames. The stench is unimaginable. Lacking water to drink, there is certainly none for washing, let alone for scrubbing the floors where people have vomited or helplessly emptied their bowels.

Desperate, the reverend chants passages from scripture: "Until the Ancient of Days came, and judgment was given to the saints of the Most High; and the time came that the saints possessed the kingdom... Ye shall see the Son of Man sitting on the right hand of power, and coming in the clouds of heaven."

Not being among the saints, the import of all this escapes me, and besides, what is the quality of the power he prophesied, now that even the saints are dying? In fact, the saints are dying more quickly than the general population.

It is too late for consolation, but the reverend chants on and on to the few who will listen. The reverend has not lost his entire congregation to the ravages of doubt; there is a small group remaining in the facility whose faith is unshaken. Yet, to be fair to the intellectual integrity of those faithful few, most have no strength to do otherwise. He counts among the faithful the people who have totally lost their minds. Some are going to remain in the facility after the inevitable mutiny, not because they dispute the facts as presented by the mutineers—that to stay is suicide—but because they have no will in their broken hearts that moves them.

Camille is among their number. She rocks back and forth, singing old hymns and nursery rhymes to her dead daughter. When she stares out at the clouds in the valley, even if it is the Son of Man she is seeing, the vision does not brighten her spirit. And apart from the singing she says nothing. I have no medicine to offer her that might cure this malady. The faint-hearted die.

There are six tourists—the reverend's last ditch converts—that he also counts as part of the faithful remnant. These people simply see no new options. They are refugees twice over already. In fact, because they survived as scavengers in Kalawao they would probably do better to leave with the mutineers. They might even be able to provide some leadership to the group and give them some pointers from their previous experience. But they insist on remaining in the facility at any cost and perhaps their reluctance to leave indicates the minimal likelihood of the mutineers' survival.

If I had tried to explain to the residents in Mahele the dimensions of the disaster in the quarantined area it might only have compounded their fear and anger. Instead, I begged them to bring more water and food, and I organized the inmates, those who were able, to make nightly trips to the ocean for wash water. That is all I could do. Caught between the two groups, I am vulnerable to criticism and suspicion from both sides. Increasingly I feared becoming the focus of the tension. I had to withdraw.

It was, however, with some sadness that I left the facility. Those people were the first people with whom I felt comfortable since I arrived on Kaane twenty years ago. I cannot explain why. I will not betray them.

Demographic survey updated:

It is now clear that few people, if any, remain in the Kalawao area of the island. This brings the total population of the island down to approximately 18,000, assuming that there has been no unreported outbreak of disease up on the mountain. Children and elderly people were most affected by the initial fallout and we have already suffered the worst of the short-term effects. The only other short-term effects still to be discovered will be among the population of pregnant women who are still carrying. Actually, we are now only talking about two or three pregnant women, to the best of my knowledge, since most pregnancies have resulted in spontaneous abortions or still-birth. My colleagues have reported no recent pregnancies, nor have they had more success than I in saving the mothers or babies in pregnancies that date back before April. In fact, Jan Ito might now be the only one still carrying. I will investigate this when I leave my house.

Notes on returning home:

As I travelled the several miles between the athletic facility and my home, I couldn't help but look up toward the brown blemish on the peak of Halepele, the crater that had been the satellite tracking station. Had I put my mind to it at all, I think I'd have imagined a war fought with missiles to be sterile and clean, and I would have imagined the world, after the war, resembling the surface of the moon. No pain. No more dying. But, in fact, there is always blood. I think about the floor of the athletic facility, layer upon layer of human waste and effluvia that cannot be washed away; the filth gets deeper. To distract myself I looked up again at the site of the blast. The crater, way up on the barren peak of Halepele, stares down like a dark pupil in a glazed eye.

It struck me that the island itself is operating exactly like a hospital, and we are all performing our functions within that framework. The reverend is the pain-killer, morphine in this case, which is addictive and blinding, but who would deny morphine to a dying patient? Teri Masaoka is a good nurse. She takes care of the human details, checks bowel movements, changes the dressings, and tries to get us to rally our spirits. She knows that the determination to live is as essential as oxygen in our blood. Myself, I am a hard-working doctor on call. I do what I have been trained to do and, within the context of the ward, what I do makes good sense. But the cure for the disease, that is beyond me. It was too late before we even suspected the danger.

I stopped at the hospital on my way home. Of course it was deserted, although the doors were unlocked. On the third floor there is one small locked supplies closet. There we keep the few serums and supplies that were left or are being reserved for emergencies. This is where my bottle of penicillin is stored, mismarked purposely so as to go undetected by my colleagues. I prepared enough to cure me of any non-fatal infection I might have contracted in the facility; I took ten days' series, carefully measured out into a smaller bottle. I have no intention of dying from compassion. The larger bottle was returned to the closet and I slipped the smaller one into my pocket.

As I hurried down the corridor I noticed a shadow moving around the corner. Turning around, I stared back into the blank eyes of a soldier, one I'd never seen before. He couldn't have been more than twenty-one years old. His face was chalky-white but he had pathetic, coal-black eyes, hardly any white showing. He saluted me. I hurried out without saying a word to him.

Then, after passing through the rest of town, I entered the valley in which my home is nestled, just outside of Mahele, and cool air rushed over me. The valley is magic in its cool dampness. No wonder the Hawaiian kings claimed that it was holy and their own. By doing so they kept out the riff raff. Flowers still grow in neglected beds. I picked red blossoms, some sort of orchid with a purple spotted tongue. Nothing in my home was touched in my absence. The local people kept this promise. Their anger is under control—a good sign.

I took my first dose of penicillin hastily. I am aware that there were children who died without drugs, but I have always kept the edict: "Physician, heal thyself."

The flowers from the garden are in front of me now, floating in a bowl. Their shadows swim across the bottom of the bowl.

13

For three weeks Steven's pants, stained with his mother's blood, hung over the chair in his bedroom. They'd been there since the day he'd helped carry his mother, bleeding and unconscious, up from the taro paddies. This morning, just as he'd done every morning since that day, he stared at the blood-stained pants, fidgeting with the loose strings that hung from the edge of his bedspread. Then he crawled out of bed and into the living room where Michael and Tomi were cooking breakfast. Michael placed a pot of rice over the fire.

"Steven," Michael said, "morning."

"Good morning," Steven muttered.

"Teri's coming today to see Mom," Tomi said. "Dad's just making us all breakfast. Frosted flakes," Tomi started the game, grinning playfully.

"Animal crackers," Michael said.

"Sugar Puffs," Tomi said.

"Alphabits," Michael said. He and Tomi looked at Steven.

"It's your turn, Steven," Tomi prodded.

"I'm not playing that dumb game," Steven grunted. He slumped onto the sofa, curling his legs up to his chest, his eyes squinting in the bright daylight, his shoulders curving as his head sunk onto his knees. Tomi shrugged.

From her bed Jan listened to her family preparing breakfast. She didn't move. She didn't have to do anything. The muffled sounds were intimate, warm; they seemed to embrace her as she lay back on the pillows. Michael's voice sounded deep and firm and even, a distant rumble from the next room, and it comforted her.

During the three weeks that Jan had spent in bed, Michael had tended the garden and the cow while the boys did the cooking, hauled the washing water, boiled the drinking water, and tended the fire. Jan would prop herself up against the headboard to accept their offerings: oatmeal, potatoes, an occasional egg donated by one of the neighbors. She was settling in and the panic that had been the source of her driving energy since April had subsided. Now she felt resigned. She would wait.

Receiving gifts from neighbors was turning out to be quite a pleasant experience. It was new to her, this "Oh, it's so kind of you to bring us cooking oil. Where did you get it?" The grateful words tripped off her tongue and surprised her. Jan noticed that everyone liked her more now that she owed them something.

Teri was on the road up-country that morning. She came up to Lono every five or six days to check on Jan. Now that Bea was gone, Teri's workload had become onerous. The strain was showing. She and Koken had started arguing over her work; this very morning they'd had a row. It began simply enough. She asked Koken if he would do the gardening, weeding out a row or two, picking off the bugs, hauling water for seedlings. He'd gone into a rage, told her she was abandoning him, putting everyone else's problems first, that they themselves might starve if she kept it up.

"And what about the tower," he'd shouted at her. "When am I suppose to work on the tower?"

Koken's reactions were incomprehensible to Teri. These days, with only a few women still carrying their babies, she had to offer them whatever help she could. Without babies the island would begin withering from inside itself. But Koken's face went blank and his body rigid when she said these things. Eventually, she met his resistence with her own silence.

Teri shook her head, and had finished packing a bag to take up-country.

When she arrived at Jan's with a backpack loaded with food, Michael met her at the door. She unloaded the pack in the front hall and handed him some bundles. "There's the obstetrics books you wanted to look at," she said. "How is Jan?"

"Just go on in," he said, pointing toward the bedroom.

"Oh, there's some notes and some more some drawings Koken wanted you to look at in that pack too. They're stuck in the book," Teri added.

Teri tried to straighten her shoulders before she went into the bedroom, leaving Michael behind with the drawings—diagrams of the tower—which he was spreading across the table. Jan was dozing off, but she woke up when she heard Teri come in. "Well, it's the good fairy," Jan said, glad for the visitor.

"Hi. How's it going?" Teri asked.

"Fine, but oh, Teri, I'm bored."

Teri's glance shifted, and the weight she felt, having tried to shrug it off before she came in to see Jan, began pulling her down again. She didn't remember what it was like to be bored, and Jan, recognizing the irritated expression that had crossed Teri's face, felt a pang of guilt. "Hey, I've been thinking..."

"Did you take your temperature this morning?" Teri interrupted, putting her hand on Jan's forehead.

"It's normal," Jan said. "Teri, I thought of an idea. Maybe I should start sewing things for people. I could do it in exchange for all their goodies that you bring me. What do you think?"

"I think you look wonderful." Teri began to fuss over Jan, pulling her sheets tight around her. Sitting down on the edge of the bed she plumped up a pillow. "And I also think you should keep rested instead of opening up business as a seamstress. Has the baby been kicking today?"

"Just a minute ago. Do you want to feel it?"

"Yeah, let's have a look at this amazing belly."

Jan lifted up her night shirt so that Teri could palpate the baby. Teri put the stethoscope Bea had given her on Jan's belly and checked the baby's heartbeat against her watch. "Very good," she said to Jan. It amazed Teri, the regularity of this baby's heartbeat, and its size. Everything seemed so normal.

"How are the other women doing? You're the whole island's midwife now, I hear."

"I won't be your midwife for long. Your husband is working toward the position. He had me bring over all my books."

"You're kidding."

"I'm not."

Jan looked away from Teri, recognizing that Teri had changed the subject. She never answered Jan's questions about the others, but then Jan never pressed her. She didn't really want to know about the other women. What do they have to do with me? she thought. Teri continued massaging her abdomen.

"So, what do you think?" Jan asked.

"I think you are doing very well, and baby here is strong and getting big. Have you been getting up at all?"

"Just wandering around the house now and again." Jan looked sheepish. "Well, once I went out just to check on the seedlings. Don't tell Michael. He and the boys are working so hard. I don't want them thinking I don't trust them. But those seedlings are so important."

"And how were they doing?"

"Fine. Most of them have their first set of true leaves now. The beans are doing best, but they always do. And the shade screen is working wonderfully."

"See. The boys can take care of them, and Michael is doing fine with the garden, so you can stay in bed." She pulled Jan's nightgown back down, and Jan tucked it in around her legs, having accepted Teri's reprimand. Teri was right; Michael and the boys deserved her trust; they were doing very well.

Still, Jan's arms and legs ached to move again. "How long will I have to stay here?" she asked Teri.

"Probably as long as you're pregnant."

Jan groaned. It was impossible for her to stay in bed three more months, particularly now that she was feeling so well. The family couldn't survive on charity that long and the boys would be worked to death. Still, she hesitated before she confronted Teri.

"Look, Teri," Jan started. "In a way I've enjoyed this. I'm liking it, believe it or not, but it isn't right. The world's upside down. There's so much to do."

"Do you have a plan that will set the world upside right?"

Jan smiled, "I could help with the taro."

"Listen, you are about six months along now, is that what you figure?"

"About that, maybe seven."

"Well," Teri's voice lowered. "You know what has happened with most of the pregnant women."

"It's not the same with this baby," Jan mumbled, hoping Teri wouldn't go on.

Teri ignored Jan's statement. "Most of them haven't been able to carry their babies even as long as you already have. There is no back up equipment now, no incubators, nothing. If you miscarry we'll be lucky if we can save you; forget the newborn. So how bad do you want this baby?"

"Enough that I'll stay in bed until it is born."

"Well, then you better."

Jan fell back into her pillows. "Okay. Do you have any other news?"

"We're all very proud of you."

"Oh, good," Jan wrinkled her nose.

"Look, I'm sorry," Teri said, knowing Jan didn't understand the facts. "But the longer you hold on, the better the baby's chances are for survival and the better yours are as well. We don't know what's happening with this baby or why you started bleeding. My advice to you is that you stay in bed, but you have to make up our own mind about what you want to do."

"Why doesn't anyone know anything?" Jan pouted.

"Because this never happened before," Teri snapped. A blush heated her cheeks when she heard herself say that, but she couldn't help it anymore; Jan's childish questions were getting too painful to listen to. She had never thought of Jan as naive before.

"Clean sheets," Jan said.

"What?"

"It's the game. Your turn, Teri."

"I don't have time for the game today."

Jan turned her face to the window and, when she spoke after a moment, her voice sounded as though it came from somewhere far away. "I'm sorry, Teri. I'm living in this bedroom and I forget. Except for the electricity being out, and the food, it sometimes seems as if everything is back to normal. I'm just waiting for my baby and the rest of the world is ticking on like always."

Teri smiled. "It's as it should be for you, then. You stay in bed and enjoy the rest. Now, clean sheets, you said? Okay. Christmas cake."

"Santa Claus," Jan laughed.

"My car."

"The radio."

"Ultrasound," Teri said.

Jan screwed up her mouth. "Ultrasound? What on earth made you say that?" Then she looked Teri straight in the eyes. "You know, Teri, you are getting to be less and less fun to play with."

"Sorry, Jan." Teri leaned over to tuck the sheets in again. "I'm out of sorts today, that's all. I'd better just be on my way. Hey, I'm headed toward the taro paddies. Is there anything you need next time I'm around? Anything you want to tell the other women?" She got up to go.

"Oh, Teri. Play the game some more, just for a minute. The day is so long. Please? Where were we? Clean sheets?"

"Okay. Hiking boots," Teri said.

"You miss hiking boots? You never used to wear hiking boots."

"I never hiked before. I do now, and I miss them. It's your turn."

"Letters. I miss letters from my family."

"I have to go."

"Oh, please play."

"Okay. Bea. I miss Dr. Bea."

"I can't believe it. How can anyone miss Dr. Bea?"

"She's a good woman. She does what she can."

"Yeah? She sure misses the mark," Jan frowned.

"We need her. Your baby needs her."

"Well, where the hell is she then? I guess Dr. Bea starts seeming fine by comparison now, now that everyone's run short on good will, huh?"

"We're getting nowhere with our game, and I have to go." Teri turned away.

"You know, Teri, why is it? I used to think the big problem was that things get broken. You know, no matter how careful we are things always break. But now I think, even more so there's the problem that we run short, we come up short. Not just now; even before. You know what I mean?"

Teri sighed. "No. But listen, I do have to go. Is there something you want me to tell anyone? I won't be back this way for a few more days."

"Tell them I had a dream that my baby is a girl. I did have this dream, Teri. I dreamed about these hands—God's hands, I think—

and they delivered the baby, and it was a girl. Beautiful hands." Jan clasped her own hands together and rested them on her belly. "Tell them it was perfect, that everything will be fine."

This strange flood of words from Jan swept away Teri's carefully constructed optimism. Jan's was the self-centered knowledge of pregnancy, the unlimited possibilities of the unborn, and Teri couldn't listen to it. Still, Teri resolved, no one could take that away from Jan; no one would.

"I'll tell them about your dream," Teri said.

Then Jan felt embarrassed. "You tell them that and they'll know I've lost my mind," she laughed. "But tell them anyway."

"I will. Bye now," and Teri went around the bed to kiss Jan goodbye. It felt awkward, but Teri needed her friend's touch. Jan's forehead warmed Teri's lips.

"How is she?" Michael said as Teri came into the kitchen.

"Fine."

"The truth?"

"She's doing all right. The baby seems to be fine too."

Michael smiled and poured Teri some tea. To him, the fetus' life and his own seemed to hang in the same balance. "Our baby is going to live," he said. "It's fine."

Teri nodded. "Sure it will be fine. And Jan's going to be fine. Let me have that tea."

Michael handed her the cup, and they sat down. Michael had drawn up a list of tasks, as they'd done every week since Jan was put to bed, a list of what they had to do and what they could get from neighbors. Large tasks they broke down into many small ones. Nothing was too big a problem to manage if they could avoid looking at the whole.

Steven was standing in the doorway, listening. "Did you say Mom's going to stay in bed for three more months? Sure thing," he said, sceptical.

Teri turned toward him. "Steven, we'll work it out. People will have to give us a hand, but it'll work out."

Tomi popped out from behind Steven's back and squeezed his way into the kitchen. "Is Mom going to be okay?"

"Sure, honey," Teri said. "But you're going to have to keep

helping us around here."

"No problem!" Tomi said.

Steven rolled his eyes. "No problem? You dummy. All the work around here and you say 'No problem'."

"Steven, water the seedlings before you go hunting," Michael interrupted as he got to his feet. "Tomi, give him a hand."

"Ah, Dad," Tomi whined.

"Steven, why don't you try to get that pheasant today?" Teri said. "Your mother could do with some meat. Or how about a wild boar?"

"Or tuna fish," Tomi smiled.

"Lake trout," said Michael.

"Ravioli," said Tomi.

Teri laughed and took her turn. "Barbecue spare ribs."

"Shit," Steven mumbled and walked out the front door.

All the way to the taro patch Teri considered Jan's question: Why doesn't anyone know anything? She wondered if she was being fair, not telling Jan what everyone did know. Last week another woman, eight months pregnant, had died, and Teri had examined the deformed fetus. Then there had been a new wave of children's deaths and no one knew why. In the compound new diseases were spreading. Facts and storytelling were becoming indistinguishable. Teri wished Bea would send a message, tell her what was happening.

The locals' weren't the only recent deaths, either. No one seemed to know why the soldiers were dying, not that anyone really cared, so long as they stayed away. But Teri was beginning to understand something. It seemed that everyone was now treating their life like an oyster treats a grain of sand that is lodged in its shell, coating it to dull the irritation, coating it over again and again to a hard gem. Everyone was becoming more isolated, more private. Even Koken was getting harder, quieter.

Before April Koken hadn't minded working around the house, putting in a vegetable garden, or hunting and fishing with some of the other men. Sometimes he and his buddies went over to the beaches to fish and harvest seaweed like their grandfathers had taught them as boys, but now the men were going to the beach alone, if at all. And Koken spent most of his time now working on the mechanisms for the tower, rubbing grease off old parts.

Now there was often only silence between Koken and Teri. In the evening she read and he worked with the tubes and wires until the darkness was too thick and the candles burned down. His coolness toward her didn't make sense to her; she was doing her best with what they had. Last night she found a gun under his work bench.

Teri thought it might be best if she just left Koken alone. Maybe he was right about the radio tower. Maybe they would reach someone. At night she looked onto the water and the darkness seemed impenetrable. Most of the time she was convinced there was nothing out there, that Koken's work on the tower was a game he played with the truth, but how could she know for sure? She couldn't be sure.

14

"It will bring in more visitors. It's lonely here, you know," Jan pouted. She had begun taking in sewing and was fending off objections, pointing out that she could manage it from her bed. "And," she added, "I'm restless."

Michael shook his head in disbelief. Neither he nor Teri believed Jan anymore when she complained. Her skin had turned the texture and color of pale orchids; she looked too good to be lonely. In the end, Teri had relented and helped Jan organize the project, telling the women at the taro paddies that Jan would do their sewing in exchange for food, and she began to bring Jan mending. It was impossible to resist Jan.

During her second month of confinement Jan had also worked out a system of lights that flashed out messages between the houses up and down the mountain. The lights worked like Morse code; she'd seen the system in a movie. Michael repaired the generator and rigged up a recharger for the flashlight batteries. He carefully poured just enough gasoline into the generator to do the job, and now in the evenings lights were blinking short messages from one house to the next from up on Lono down to Mahele. Now the darkness was not an enemy that kept people huddled in their houses; it became the medium of quick communications, the lights blinking out messages when someone was sick, when someone had fish to trade for vegetables, when someone wanted company. Every family in the taro project had a flash code. The children loved it. They were the keepers of the lights.

The generator and the system of recharging the batteries provided the Ito family with a guarantee that they would remain in good favor with the neighbors, who arrived regularly to recharge their batteries and drop off their mending. Each visitor would bring some offering of fresh food for the family as well, and, between the generator and the sewing, the family was able to break even with its neighbors.

Day after day Jan spent, propped up in bed on her pillows, sewing mounds of cloth. Embroidery, spots of applique, and careful patches turned old things into new things. Jan fingered the cloth bits. Her scissors clipped out a rhythm. Some tiny scraps were secured and quilted into new baby's clothes. Those were Jan's passion. Size one seemed like a half-forgotten dream, but her fingers remembered as she shaped the pink scraps into a minute nightshirt, a bonnet, and some little dresses.

It was in Jan's sewing for her new baby that the child began forming itself in Jan's imagination. She was determined it was a girl, favoring pink scraps of cloth and quilting them in patterns and shades that ranged from almost-red to white. Jan decided that it would be a serious child, so she would forgo ruffles on the small dresses. Jan felt the child would be practical, so she sewed small bibs to cover the baby's shirts. And, convinced that her child would be beautiful and graceful, Jan checked to be sure the hems were straight, and along the edges she worked in some fine embroidery.

One morning, as Jan was sorting buttons, sewing matching buttons onto individual cards, she was pulled out of her reverie when she heard the front door open. Michael was expected back, and she called, "Michael, is that you?"

No answer. A moment later Jan heard footsteps in the hall outside her room. "Michael?"

Camille stood there in the bedroom doorway. Thin, bleeding cuts on her hands and legs were visible through the dirt coating her skin. Her clothes were torn, and entangled in her hair were bits of weed.

"You're the one," Camille whispered.

Jan shifted nervously on the bed. She pulled the blanket over herself and tried to speak calmly. "Well, Camille, how have you been? I haven't seen you in weeks."

"You're the mother of the one who is to come," Camille chanted again.

"Oh, my baby's due in another month—well, two months at the most, Camille." Jan heard her own voice sounding weak. "We haven't chosen a name yet. I think it's going to be a girl. Did you want to see the baby clothes I've been sewing?" She held up a few tiny garments.

Camille didn't look at the clothing. She repeated, "Your baby is the one." Then she turned and was gone.

"Camille, wait!" Jan shouted, and tried to raise herself out of bed. Her legs were asleep and the prickling stung them as she swung them over the side of the bed. Her body began trembling, a warning sign. She looked down at her feet. They looked so far away. To Jan they felt like dead stumps of an old tree. Then she remembered that someone had told her that Camille had returned with the congregation. Michael had told her that the adventure had gone particularly badly for Camille. The congregation had been exposed to some illness and was staying at the athletic facility for a little while, just to be on the safe side, just to be sure they wouldn't spread any illness. That's why Bea was there, just to be sure. But bits of news are slow to arrive here at the house, Jan thought. Maybe I've misunderstood. Holy God, what is wrong with Camille? she wondered. The woman looks like hell.

Jan's legs slowly stopped tingling and, as she sat in the quiet of her bedroom, she wondered if the entire episode might have been her own imagining; she had spent so much time alone. No. Camille had really stood there. She had said something, something like "You're baby is the one."

Camille's words themselves hadn't frightened Jan. They echoed in her memory, stirring an idea, resounding with something she already knew. I am going crazy from being in bed so long, she concluded. No matter what, I have to get up. I can just go into the garden for a moment; breath the air in the garden; check on the plants. Then I'll come right back into bed and no one will know.

Jan flexed her toes. They moved now and Jan tested her weight on her feet. They held it. She walked slowly across the room, then through the hall to the front door. It had been left open. She walked out onto the porch and leaned against the railing to catch her breath. She filled her lungs with as much air as she could pull in and started gingerly down the five stairs to the ground.

There's a chaise lounge out back, she thought. I could just lie down back there for a moment. She headed around toward the back garden, walking through the carport. Suddenly she stopped, her eyes widening as she saw a patch of dead grass.

The generator was gone. Someone had stolen the generator. She put her hand out against the wall to steady herself, then shuffled forward into the back yard, to get to the shed in the gully, panicky, wondering whether the gasoline was still there.

She'd taken only a few steps, when she heard Michael at the front door. "Michael, I'm out here," she shouted to him. "Help me."

"What the hell are you doing up?" he snapped.

"Quick. Go to the shed and check if the gasoline is still there."

"What are you talking about? You sit down. Here. Here's the chaise. Now sit down." He helped her onto the lounge chair, and Jan let herself be led. She knew the gas was gone. Her hands gripped the arms of the lounge chair and her knuckles were white.

"Do you think the soldier's stole it, Michael?"

"No. Well, maybe," he mumbled.

She looked up at him. "Did you take it?"

"You mean the generator?"

Jan went pale. "Of course I mean the generator. And the gasoline."

"Well, yeah. I was going to tell you about that. It's for the communications tower. Just for a short time. It's just out on loan."

"When were you going to tell me?"

"When you asked, I guess."

"And how are you going to return the gasoline? It might be the last there is on the island."

Michael didn't look apologetic. Jan's anger took him back into his silence. He hunched his shoulders, hostile, and she saw him withdrawing. She knew she couldn't chase him there, so she backed down herself. "Okay, you tell me. How are you going to return the gasoline? Have you been drilling for oil around here? What's the plan?" She tried to laugh but failed.

"Talk to me, Michael. You can't go back on that," she said in the silence that was growing between them.

"Suppose the tower works," Michael finally answered.

"And suppose not."

"Then we're out of luck."

"And we should just curl up and die?"

"Gasoline won't save us," Michael stated flatly.

"Well, it sure helps. It means we have a communication system going here."

"Child's play."

"It's something."

"It's nothing." Glaring at her, he got up and picked up the sack he'd brought home. He pulled out a catch of fish he'd got in a trade for some lettuce and peas. A parrot fish flopped onto the grass.

Jan knew she had lost. There was no use going on about it. "Could you take me back to bed?" she asked quietly.

"Here. Lean against my shoulder." Without another word, they moved slowly around the house and up the porch steps. In the bedroom he pushed away the pile of shirts to make room for Jan on the bed. The sunlight was fading into a soft glow through the window, but Jan's face, which had softened with the month of rest, now looked slack and lifeless.

Her body had started trembling with small, involuntary spasms, but she tried to control her limbs and her voice. "Do you have any idea when the kids will be getting back?" she asked.

"Any time now, I suspect. It's getting late."

"I don't want them to see me like this. Hold me, Michael." She touched his arm lightly with her fingertips. If he would hold her she could let go of her fury. "Michael, would you make love to me?"

She pushed her hair away from her face and Michael stared at her, trying to understand her, but he couldn't hear her asking him to hang on to her, to call her back to life.

"Teri said that it isn't safe," he said.

"We wouldn't have to tell Teri," she said.

Michael still looked cross.

"Okay," she gave in. "But I'm telling you, Michael, I'm losing ground. I'm slipping."

"What can I do?" he asked.

"Talk, Michael."

"About what?"

"Anything. Just talk. Talk."

Michael was lost.

"Just talk to me, Michael. Don't stop talking," she insisted.

"Okay. Okay," he laughed nervously. "Let's play the game."

"I don't want to play the game."

"What do you want to talk about?"

"Talk about when you were a kid."

Michael's eyes rolled. "I can't."

"Please."

Michael tried to laugh. "How many times have you asked me to go on about when I was a kid?"

"I like to listen to it," she said and leaned into the pillows. His voice would make her body stop shaking; she was sure of that. She fiddled with the edge of the blanket. "You know, Mike, how I used to demand that you start talking again? I wanted you to speak to me so much, but then I began to understand. Now I only wish I could stop talking so I could speak to you."

"What do you want me to talk about?"

"Anything."

"What? Tell me what you want to hear."

"Talk about when you were a kid."

"Again?"

"Again."

Michael smiled and took her hand, settling back into the pillows next to her.

This story-telling had become a ritual between them since Michael began speaking again. Each time Michael added something, some small detail from further back in his past, from more secret places. He described the fields near their old home on Oahu and Jan could imagine playing there herself. He described his school, the short pants he wore, the crayons and colored chalks he was given, and the Mickey Mouse ABC's. He described his parents' pride in every little achievement. "Study son. Study," he was told. Their son was going to be the educated one. "Study, son. Do you want some Coke? Finish that exercise there and I'll get you some Coke with ice." He wasn't going to have to take anything from the foreman when he grew up, not their boy. His parents gave him everything they could get their hands on; they worked like dogs for him. He described the fields again.

"Do you really want to hear all this?" he asked, feeling Jan's cold fingers entwined around his. He noticed that she wasn't shaking anymore, but he wasn't sure she was listening to him.

"Just keep going," she said.

"Not now," Michael muttered and his eyes teared imperceptibly.

Jan put her hand up to her mouth. "I'm sorry, Michael." They both sat in the silence for a moment before Michael spoke again.

"Do you think about them much? Your own family?" Michael murmured, taking her hand and drawing a light circle on the back of her hand with his index finger. His voice was tentative. He didn't want her to begin trembling again, but in the intimate light of early evening it seemed everything between them would be shared. "Jan, a thousand times I've been mad at myself that I didn't help you get back to see them all these years."

"For the most part I've shut it all off. I don't think about it," she replied.

The quiet settled more deeply into the room as they held each other, curled up on the bed, until they spoke to each other in whispers.

"Do you remember me talking about Frank William? Here's a new story for you," Michael started. Jan shook her head, no, he hadn't told her the story before, and she brought the back of his hand up against her lips.

"Frank was a mover and shaker in the firm I worked for in Seattle. He and I were buddies. We used to go out for drinks together after work, that sort of thing. Well, I was working on this new engine cooling system. It was a different area than his, so it wasn't like we were in competition or anything. But one day I showed him this drawing I'd been working on, a small innovation in the system. I thought it was clever. I was proud of it, I guess. He didn't take much notice, didn't say anything one way or the other. I eventually abandoned the idea myself. Really, it would have been more suited to another project. I went to work on another project altogether a year later." He looked at Jan, who had her eyes closed now, but he knew she was still listening. He continued.

"Well, Frank and me, we lost touch with each other. The only way I knew about this was that another engineer, years later, was explaining the same design to me. I said, 'Hey, that's my old plan,' and he said he got the idea from this real brilliant guy, Frank William.

I laughed. I really did. Frank was doing very well for himself. He got transferred to an office in France with some military contracts. Well, by that time you and I'd been married and moved here." Michael checked to see if Jan was asleep. She had gotten very calm and still, gazing out the window.

"Then there was all that talk about a war," Michael went on in barely more than a whisper. "When we heard about the missiles in Europe, all I could think was that Frank William was going to go up in a mushroom cloud with my plan. Can you believe it? What a thing to haunt me. Maybe it's just that he was the only person I knew who lived in Europe." It was incomprehensible to Michael, even as he spoke, and in his mind's eye he saw only a confusing mass of images, defeats, and triumphs all melting into nothing.

Jan hunted for words but there weren't any more things for them to say to each other. They watched the long shadows made by the late, rose-colored sun.

Suddenly, Jan grinned. "Electric can openers," she said.

"Those little gummed circles you paste around the holes of notebook paper."

"Marshmallows."

"Don't get onto food. Street lights."

"Clean socks. Nylons."

"Shaving cream."

Michael squeezed her hand, grateful, and he would have gone on playing the game all night, but they heard the boys arriving, dragging the squeaky wagon up the driveway. "We're back!" the boys yelled in the front door. "It's Thanksgiving!"

Jan could see from her room that they had pots full of food with them. "Where the hell did you get that?" she called to them.

"And here's the best, Mom. A real turkey!" Tomi shouted and brought the platter into the bedroom.

Jan gasped. "I can't believe it. Where on earth did you get this feast? It must have come from another land. The boat must have come in!"

"Teri got it for us," Steven said. "She made the whole meal. Told us to meet her half-way up the mountain. So we did."

Tomi ran into the kitchen and found plates and silverware.

Michael took a cloth from the cupboard and draped it over the dresser. Pans were uncovered, potatoes, relishes, squash, salad, rolls, dressing and gravy. They pulled the white meat from the breast and ate with their fingers, laughing but hardly speaking between mouthfuls. Congealed gravy dripped down their chins. Once in a while Michael and Jan's eyes met. The generator was forgotten; the food was healing them.

Once they had filled their bellies, they put some of the meat on the fire to reheat, thinned the gravy, fried the potatoes, and began eating again. "Is this great, or what?" Steven mumbled with his mouth full.

"More dressing over here," Jan said.

It took over an hour, but eventually they stopped eating. As the noise of eating lessened, talk filled in the empty places, simple talk from filled bellies. Little stories from the day were related. What was going on with Teri? Was the water level in the well rising? Simple talk.

There was even pumpkin pie. Michael suggested they take it out on the deck and watch the last of the sunset. "You think you're up for another hike?" Michael asked Jan. "I could carry you."

"You think you're up for that?" Jan laughed.

"Oh God, you are a tub of lard," Michael grunted, supporting her weight.

From the deck they could see out over the harbor. The ocean was calm, and the colors of the sunset reflected off the water. They listened for animal noises, but only the cow's lowing broke the stillness. Tomi coaxed Jan, "Mommy, please sing."

"Oh, Steven, you and Tomi sing one of your old cub scout songs," she encouraged them. Steven flinched and his mother recognized the movement in his shoulder. She had belittled him again, accidentally. She tried to make amends. She turned to Tomi. "Okay, Tomi, it's just you and me."

Tentatively at first, Tomi and Michael joined in as she led an old song from around her family's campfires thousands of miles away. "Found a peanut, found a peanut, found a peanut just now. I just now found a peanut, found a peanut just now." Finally Steven joined in. Out into the darkness the four of them sang songs until it was past time for bed.

15

December 3

Epidemic:

The survivors in the athletic facility disbanded after Reverend Tompson died early last week. Evidently, the infection responsible for most of the deaths in the congregation proved fatal for him as well. With the disbanding of the quarantined group, the spread of the disease is beyond the control of the small medical team of which I am a part. My colleagues and I are trying to trace the spread of infection— believing it to be typhus or a typhoid-like bacteria—in the hopes of reinstating some sort of quarantine program. The graphs I made several months ago, to study the disease that was presumably caused by fallout, will be immensely useful now, since the areas previously affected are now most prone to disease, and because the graphs are geographically precise.

The number of persons from the facility who are now at large is twenty-three, all suspected carriers of the infection. It appears that some families have harbored members of the congregation, because the families themselves have contracted the disease. Many people in a small apartment block in the Mahele area are affected, as well as some students in the college residence. I have suggested that these two buildings be turned into sub-units of the hospital to prevent the disease from spreading further.

The hospital has been reopened, staffed by members of the patients' families, since these people are already exposed and are the most highly motivated to carry out what little treatment we can offer. The treatment consists of the provision of a high protein diet with plenty of liquids, bed rest, and fever control. The relatives of the patients offer each other relief and help prepare the food in bulk. So the hospital acts as an unofficial quarantine, which I endorse. However, the less said by me throughout this period, the better.

I am back to work, but my effectiveness is not what it could have been had I remained in the athletic facility and attempted to prevent this mutiny. Some people say that the congregation should have been shot and they hold me responsible for the congregation's actions. They blame me for setting a bad example in the quarantined area, having broken the quarantine myself. Yet my conscience is clear. They simply don't understand that medical personnel routinely move in and out of quarantined areas. We are trained to take meticulous precautions to prevent the spread of infection, and I have never behaved negligently in this practice. They say that, by not staying in the athletic facility through to the end, I have done more harm than had I done nothing. Mind you, their judgment is made with the benefit of hindsight.

Once again the soldiers have assigned themselves a task. They are now conducting a search for the people who left the facility. They are meandering around the island, worrying the locals with their menacing habit of carrying guns. If, under any circumstances whatsoever, they were to use a gun against a local person it would be certain death for all remaining soldiers. The local people have let their imaginations run away with them on this matter. The soldiers would be well advised to watch their manners very closely. I understand they are down a few more heads already.

Camille Evans was seen most recently in the taro paddies near Ahupuaa, but when none of the women would approach her she ran away. It is rumored that her husband has taken her in, which means he and their remaining two children are at risk, as well as their neighbors in Lono. Certainly time is running out for Camille.

It is too early yet to positively diagnose cases of the disease beyond those cases detected among the congregation and those cases in Mahele. The people who have contracted it might remain asymptomatic perhaps for one more week. Reports of symptomatic illness, shortness of breath, fever, generalized weakness, and bad coughs, are coming in at an alarming rate.

Reported cases of the disease, since the return of the congregation to the Mahele area, stand at approximately 170.

16

"I'm going out for a few hours," Michael said.

"So early? Come on, curl up with me here, love, for just a bit longer. What's the hurry?" Jan asked.

"What's the problem with me going out for a few hours?"

"Nothing."

"It's a meeting."

"What about?"

"Food."

"Oh."

When they passed each other on the road, the men living around Lono had talked about organizing themselves so that they could take turns making the trip down the mountain and back. As it was, each one of them was going alone every week or two, and bringing back a small amount fish and seaweed that they had traded for the food they were growing up-country. If the new plan worked, one of them in turn would only have to go down to the beach once a month and would bring back enough fish and seaweed to distribute to the neighbors.

Two weeks ago they'd decided to call a meeting to discuss the plan, but now that the time for the meeting had come, an epidemic had broken out, and they were more scared than hungry. Michael had gone partway down the mountain to meet Koken and give him some parts for the transmitter, but that was the only risk he'd take. No one was going down-country, not even to fish. People living up-country weren't anxious for visitors either, or even for food for that could be brought up the mountain, for fear it was contaminated.

Michael felt badly, admitting this fear even to himself. After all, the congregation had consisted largely of people from their neighborhood. It was the upwardly-mobile professionals who inhabited these higher, cooler slopes of Halepele, and it was many of these same people who had made up the congregation of the Church of Jesus Christ, just outside of Lono. But by lucky chance, the believers were not up here any longer. They were down by the beaches, probably spreading out in the wooded area in the valley, hiding and scrounging and dying, and the neighbors up in Lono wanted things to remain just as they were, with a fragile seven miles of mountain barrier protecting the lucky ones from the unlucky ones.

Most of the people up-country could be trusted not to harbor members of the congregation, trusted to maintain the barrier, but there were rumors that Ralph was desperate, that he wanted his wife, Camille, back home to take care of the two boys, and that he'd taken steps to find her. He'd be there today, Michael knew, at Charlotte and Alex's house where the meeting was called; he'd be there to get in on the plan. Ralph was desperate.

Michael was right; Ralph did come to the meeting and sat, fidgeting nervously with the loose skin around his throat, on the edge of the discussion. His eyes shifted over the crowd in the living room. Occasionally someone's eyes would rest on Ralph and the color rose in his cheeks. If someone was going to accuse him, they'd have to say the words to his face, because obviously he wasn't budging until they did.

The room became quiet when the neighbors got anxious to begin. The man who sat in the front row of the lawn chairs that were set out in rows across Charlotte and Alex's living room stood up and asked for silence.

"The way I see it," he said, "we have one main problem to solve here: the soldiers. We've got to be careful with those guys, with them trekking up and down the mountain. They could carry this disease and God knows what else. And for another thing, they might use this opportunity to steal from our gardens, take the cows, whatever. They know we're afraid to go chasing them down the mountain, and that fear makes us vulnerable."

"Yeah, yeah," several other men shouted agreement.

"Hey, I thought we were going to talk about food, about getting fish," Charlotte said loudly to her husband, Alex.

"You got it. We need our own defence plan, regular patrols," the man by the window called out, ignoring Charlotte. "First to protect ourselves from the soldiers should they get cocky and begin looting around here. Second, to patrol the area so those carriers down-country don't come by this way."

"You mean people from the congregation? My wife, for example?" The sound of Ralph's voice unnerved the group. He rose to his feet. "I know what you all are thinking, so I'm going to tell you: it's not true. I'm not keeping Camille at our house." His eyes travelled around the room. "She come around all right, but I wouldn't let her in, not after she killed my daughter. And that's the way I see it. With all her foolishness, dragging Susan across the island, Camille might as well have shot her point-blank. She killed my daughter." He coughed and rubbed his eye with his closed fist. "So you don't have to worry about me. I won't have my younger kids exposed so she can kill them too. So you can just quit staring at me like that, like I would."

His voice trailed off, and no one spoke. Ralph was angry, not grieving, so there was no need to comfort him. In fact, everyone basically agreed with him; Camille was a killer.

"That underscores my point," the man standing by the window said. "We need a system of defence."

"Ah, come on. No one has time for regular patrols or anything like that," another man spoke up. "We need to rely on people overlooking their immediate areas. We've always done that for each other. That's just being neighbors."

"Well, everyone has flashlights, am I right?" a woman asked, standing up in the middle of the room. The others nodded. "So if anything happens at night, say a soldier is prowling in your back yard, then you can signal some neighbors for help."

"Right." Everyone agreed.

"I don't think anyone should take on even one soldier alone," another woman said.

"No, you're right," the first woman agreed. "Just signal your neighbors if it's at night, and in the day-time you had better just haul out of there and find some other people. We should always work at least in pairs; three or four would be best." Several people nodded.

"But what do we do if they do come up here? Say a soldier turns up and just won't leave?" Charlotte asked. She nudged her husband, Alex, who'd been a cop up until last April. "Honey, tell them about your guns."

Alex cleared his throat and stood up reluctantly. "Dear, I was going to get to that. See," he said to the crowd, "I have these two pistols. They're your standard issue police pistols. If we ever need to confront the soldiers I think we should be armed."

"After all, they are," Charlotte added.

"So let's have a volunteer to take the other one, someone from the other end of Lono, and I'll keep one at our house. Then, if you need some help you can go find one or the other of these guns." Alex looked around the room to see who would volunteer.

"I'll take it," Ralph spoke up. There was a pause before anyone spoke.

"You know how to handle a gun?" Alex asked.

"Sure, I'm from Texas, aren't I?"

"Is that okay with the rest of you?" Alex was anxious not to give Ralph the pistol, but he didn't want to be the one to say so. He scanned the room for objections. No one else wanted to be the dissenter. "Okay, then. We've got the plan worked out. If either a soldier or any other intruder shows up in this area you go get Ralph or me. And it's everyone's job to stay alert. Agreed?"

"Agreed," they mumbled.

They also agreed that they should meet again in a week to check on the sitation.

"Everybody got enough charge left in their flashlights?" someone called out. The word had spread that Michael had taken the generator down to the beach.

"If you need recharges, drop your batteries off at the house. I'll see they get down to Koken to get recharged," Michael said. He didn't want to hear any more about the generator. Somehow he'd work out a way to get the batteries passed down the mountain to Koken.

"Well, what about counting Koken and Teri Masaoka in on this plan? And maybe that lady doctor too?" a man asked. "Let's face it. We're going to need some fish brought up, and we might need a doctor. We can still work out some trading. We need the fish."

"So we're finally going to get around to talking about food," Charlotte grumbled.

"That doctor is the one who started this thing. If it weren't for her, they would have taken care of the congregation in Mahele, before the disease had the chance to spread. They wanted to; they wanted to shoot them," someone bellowed out.

"She's infected," another added.

"Look. If she was infected she'd be dead by now. We need help from down-country, and we need their fish," Alex argued.

"I don't want their fish," someone else hissed.

"We need the batteries," Alex insisted.

"Jan might need the doctor," Michael mumbled. At that, everyone hesitated a moment.

"Face it," Alex spoke. "What is it? Twenty-some families up here? We can't make it on our own."

And so it was decided that Koken and Teri would be invited to the next meeting, provided that they took care that they weren't further exposed, and they would be asked to bring some fish. Everyone came up with something that they could trade for the fish. Someone had some rubbing alcohol he'd been hoarding. Then there was the clothing that Jan had mended. And there were fresh vegetables from the gardens. That would be enough to lure the fish.

While they were setting the date for the next meeting, Charlotte realized it would be just a week before Christmas. "Maybe we could go caroling together?" she laughed.

"Okay." Ralph said. His neighbors rolled their eyes. "Oh, come on," he coaxed. "We need a good drunk."

"I need a drunk," Alex said.

"Okay. Make it a party," Michael said.

Everyone agreed, and a young man sitting in the corner announced that he was making wine that he would contribute, provided that people would trade with him for some food. He was single, so he had no claim on the produce from the taro paddies, but he was promised twenty pounds of rice from the first crop in exchange for the wine for the party. He agreed. Everyone else would bring food. That was that. They decided they'd try.

Michael looked at the faces in the room. Few locals, few like himself, were here. Teri hadn't been to see Jan since the outbreak. Perhaps it was Teri's own precaution, or perhaps Bea had insisted she not risk contaminating the family. The circle around Jan and Michael was growing tighter, choking Michael. He left the meeting for home as soon as he could slip out unnoticed. A neighbor passed him at the door and handed him a bag, whispering in a hoarse voice, "Don't open it here. A present from the Masaokas."

Jan spent the morning sewing, lying on the lounge chair by the side of the garden. It was almost time for the baby to be born anyway; she could venture out now and then, she thought, and she had talked the boys into helping her down the stairs, so she could watch them weed and water the vegetable patch. Arriving at the end of each row provided them with an excuse for a break and they'd sit next to Jan and discuss the vegetables' progress and the shape of the clouds.

"Mom, did you want me or Steven to be a girl? I mean before we were born," Tomi asked.

"No. I didn't much care."

"That's a dumb question," Steven said. "What difference does it make?"

"Well, I would have been able to wear all those pink baby clothes Aunt Jenny gave us if I'd been a girl. If I was a girl would you have made me a dress like this?" Tomi asked, holding up the tiny, white lace gown Jan had just finished.

"You did wear a dress like that," Jan laughed.

"No," Tomi shook his head.

"Oh, yes you did. Anyway, I thought you were just perfect," Jan said, winking at him.

"I wish I was a girl, still. You already had a boy."

"But then who would have been Tomi if you weren't?"

Tomi wrinkled up his nose. "Mom, you're kidding me."

"No. I was happy you were a boy."

"Then why do you want a girl now?"

"I'll take what I get. Moms are funny that way. It doesn't really matter; we like our babies just fine."

"Even if it's a monster? My friend, Jeffrey, said his mother told his dad that our baby will probably be a monster."

"Why don't you shut up, stupid," Steven said and knocked his little brother's leg with the trowel. Jan winced and looked away from the boys so they couldn't see her face. Her chin trembled.

"Sorry, Mom," Tomi mumbled.

"That's okay. Of course we think about that. But I just think, that since we don't know anything about it, maybe we can just wait and see, that everything is going to be okay."

"Yeah, let's wait and see," said Steven. "And in the meantime you can shut up, Tomi."

It certainly wasn't the first time Jan had considered the possibility that Tomi's friend might be right. Every time Teri or Bea had examined her, she in turn had examined their faces looking for any hint of something they wouldn't tell her. She had interpreted their satisfaction with her progress as a good sign. There was something special about this one. She was sure it was going to make it.

"Look, boys," she said. "The garden looks great now, and I have an idea. I think it's time we did our bit at the taro paddy. So why don't you two mosey on down there and help."

"See, Steven? I told you she wanted girls instead of us. Now she's making us do girls' work."

"Tomi, there's nothing that says men can't grow taro. You've seen those pictures of the huge, old Hawaiian men growing taro."

"I hate poi," said Steven.

"Me too," Tomi echoed.

"They say it's the food of the gods," Jan said.

"They also say God's dead," Steven added.

"And Mom says 'Get going, boys.'" Jan laughed.

"Okay. Okay." Steven said, "Come on, Tomi," and Tomi followed him into the house.

"See you later, Mom. And don't go walking around when we get out of sight. Dad will be home soon. He can help you get back to bed," Steven called out to her.

"See you later, kids. Don't worry about me." She watched the two of them troop off, Tomi with his shovel and Steven with his spear over his shoulder. The sun gleamed off the metal tools.

Jan put down her sewing and rubbed her belly, waiting for Michael to come up the driveway. She watched a gecko on a branch of the grapefruit tree. She listened for the elepaio birds in the stand of trees behind their land. The garden was so silent she thought she might hear the baby's heartbeat if she listened.

Then she saw Michael through the window, moving around the

kitchen. "I'm out here," she called to him. He waved and hurried out to her.

"Did you come out here by yourself?" Michael asked. The sack was still slung onto his back. "You know you're not supposed to try stairs by yourself..."

Jan cut him off. "The boys helped me down the stairs. Don't worry. I'm fine. Just needed some sunlight. I sent the boys to go help at the taro paddies. You must have just missed them. I didn't see you come in."

"The boys agreed to work in the paddies?"

"With a bit of argument."

Michael bit the inside of his cheek. Lately, Jan noticed, he seemed nervous whenever his sons were out of sight, but they are too old to be kept around the yard all the time, she thought. They'd never put up with that.

"Look at this haul from the beach," he said, pulling an octopus from his sack with one hand and a fistful of black seaweed with the other. "Koken had it sent up with one of the guys who was coming this way. He told me Teri says 'Hi'. She wants you to flash a message if you need her, but otherwise she's real busy in town. What do you think of this thing?" He held up the octopus like a trophy.

"It's disgusting."

"I'm cooking it up for dinner. We'll eat well tonight."

Jan marvelled at the fact that her mouth watered. It seemed every few days they had one good meal, and now their bodies were adjusting. In between they ate rice or porridge with fruit to stave off hunger pain, but then, just when it was getting bad, some good food would come in. She thought back to the old days of the supermarket. She had hated grocery shopping. Three meals a day. Nine months ago.

"Looks wonderful, Michael."

"It'll be great. How about I cook it out here on the grill? You can talk to me while I clean it up. I guess I better boil it first."

"Boil it here, but clean it over there out of my sight, please."

Michael's fingers remembered everything his father taught him about preparing the octopus. After soaking it and getting the fire started, he sat down next to his wife and began rubbing her legs.

"We also have some green mangoes," he said.

"We always have some mangoes."

"Well, it's the only fruit available now."

Jan picked at her cuticle, and started the game. "Mainland apples."

"I don't want to play," Michael said abruptly. "Anyway," he looked over and touched her leg. "I have good news. You're invited to a Christmas party. Next week. We're going. It'll do you good."

Jan leaned back, surprised. "A party? Can you imagine, a party?"

"No."

"I'm going to dress up like a queen. What should I wear? I can't believe it, a party. Do you think these legs will get me there?" It is going to be different, a voice inside her warned. Don't get excited. Hold back. Hold back. The voice infuriated Jan. She hadn't been away from the house in months. She hadn't visited, danced, partied since April. She needed this as much as food.

"Teri and Koken might be there too, so you can see Teri then if she doesn't make it up here before that," Michael said. He didn't tell her that the neighbors were trading risks, chancing the possibility that Koken or Teri or Bea could contaminate them, because if the epidemic did spread they would need their help. They were hedging their bets, but Jan wouldn't understand that. She was protected.

"What will I wear?" she wondered aloud.

"Well, you've got a week to figure that out." He leaned back on the grass.

"It's almost Christmas, can you believe it?" Jan said. Christmas. The mainland trees wouldn't be coming in by ship. The boys hadn't thought to ask for anything yet. No glitter in the store. No stores. Last year she had made twenty pounds of fruit cake. To save money, she told Michael, but she really made it because she always did. For the last fifteen years she and her mother had swapped cakes, sharing recipes, small steps on the way to achieving the perfect cake. And last year she'd made a gingerbread house as well. The kitchen had been filled with Christmas smells. And there had been a parade every year on the island, not like the ones on the mainland, not like Macy's and Hudson's, but a parade nonetheless. No snow either, but she'd always watched the old Christmas movies on television. Her favorite was *White Christmas*.

Tomi and Steven arrived at the taro patch, getting there just after a few of the women who attended the meeting had also arrived. Four other women had been digging for the last few hours, and they took a break to stretch, asking the boys about Jan and the baby. How was everything in the house? they asked the boys. Was there anything they needed? Anything?

"Mom says we should lend a hand here," Steven offered reluctantly.

"Yeah," Tomi complained.

"And you don't think you should have to," a neighbor finished Steven's sentence for him.

"Well, I don't mind doing girl's work, but I don't even like poi," Tomi said. The women laughed.

"Okay. Then why don't you go see if you can find the little ones? See what they're up to and keep them out of trouble for the next hour until we finish up here. We were just about ready to call it a day before this second shift arrived," said a woman, waving her trowel in the direction of the other women who had just begun to work.

"Don't tell Mom we didn't help then," Steven looked at her sheepishly.

"You are helping," she assured him.

"Great. Come on, Tomi."

"The kids are over in those woods somewhere. They usually play somewhere by the old reservoir," a younger woman said, pointing in the direction to the far side of the taro paddies. Tomi and Steven headed off.

The woods were shadowy, the sun slipping through the leaves, and the rotting sisal stalks blocked the way every few yards. But the boys could hear the children in the distance and they followed the sound of their playing.

"Look at this," Tomi groaned to Steven, pointing to a ditch. "Oh, gross." Steven looked over Tomi's shoulder. There was a dog's carcass lying in the ditch. It stared up at them, teeming with life. Its eyes were covered with gnats.

"Disgusting," Steven said.

"Let's get out of here," Tomi said, and bolted toward the old reservoir. It didn't take them long to catch up with the children. They found them playing by the side of the water, dragging sticks into the muck. The reservoir was filled with rotting leaves and green algae.

"God, look at that," said Steven, eyeing the muck. "Disgusting."

"Hey, what's happened here?" Tomi asked. He and Steven used to play around the reservoir themselves, but it was clean then. They'd never seen it like this. The awful stillness, since no bird or animal sounds could be heard, frightened them. The two waded in up to their ankles, grabbing the younger children's hands to pull them out.

"What are you kids doing in this muck?" Steven took over, scolding them "Have your mothers been over here to check this out?"

Twelve little sets of eyes looked up at him like they'd been caught stealing cookies. "Nope," the oldest child, who was just seven years old, offered. "They just told us not to go in over our ankles. We haven't. Honest."

Steven whispered to Tomi, "I'm going to check this out. You stay here with these kids, and make sure they don't go back into the water."

"No!" Tomi screamed at him. "Don't leave me alone."

"Go," Steven ordered. Tomi stood stiff for a moment, then darted over toward the other children.

Steven went around the edge of the old reservoir. On the other side was a clearing with more woods surrounding it. He went into the woods and counted several dead birds, a stray cat and some unidentifiable rodents at various stages of decay, lying in the small streams of water that trickled down toward the reservoir. His stomach tightened and he ran back to the children. "We're getting out of here," he hollered at them. "And don't you ever come back here again! You hear me?" The little kids fell into line behind him as he headed back to the paddies.

When they arrived back, the women looked up from their digging and stared at the children's bewildered faces. "What's the matter?" a woman asked Steven.

"You kids, head on down that way." He directed the children

toward the far side of the paddy. When they were out of earshot he turned to the women. "Something's real wrong in that reservoir. Lots of dead things." His face contorted. "That's no place for those little guys."

The women exchanged looks of alarm. "Thanks, Steven. We'll look into it," one of them said, putting her hand on his shoulder. He brushed it off.

"Come on," she said to the others. "Let's finish up here. Some of you want to get those kids home, and wash them down? Wash them down good. You go with the other kids, Steven. You wash down too."

A few of the women, the youngest children's mother's, went over to the group of little ones and started herding them away.

"Someone want to check this out with me?" the first woman asked, and though clearly no one wanted to go, an older woman followed her as she climbed up the retaining wall, and the two of them headed toward the reservoir to investigate.

17

Michael never told Jan he'd gone down-country a few days after the meeting, and he didn't tell her what he'd heard from Teri. Just as he did with every new incident, he decided that the less Jan knew the better. He'd slipped down to Mahele to get the transmitter parts to Koken. He was careful; he didn't even go inside the house, but talked to Teri through the screen door. She told him she and Koken and Bea wouldn't come to the meeting if there was any danger they'd been recently exposed; they wouldn't take risks, but with luck they'd be there. Some people felt the worst was over; perhaps the epidemic had nearly run its course. Then Michael left the parts for the tower on her porch.

"Did you hear about Ralph?" Teri had asked. Michael shook his head, no. Teri told Michael the whole story, as she'd heard it from Bea, so he wouldn't have to hear it from a stranger.

Ralph had been living alone with his two youngest sons since Camille and their daughter, Susan, left on the trip across the island to Kalawao. Ralph had had a hard time. He'd never taken care of the children before. Even for the few days Camille was in the hospital having a new baby, they'd hired a housekeeper. Ralph had complained to Teri when Camille first left for Kalawao, "I don't know how Camille handled them, and I wish to hell she'd get back here where she belongs." But at that time, he'd thought she would be away just a few days. Once he found out what had happened, he'd never mentioned Camille's name to Teri again.

Teri saw him on the road once after the congregation had returned, and she asked if there was anything she could do.

"You got your own problems," Ralph had said.

"Well, there's people around. Maybe someone could take the kids for a few days. Then you could get to the beach to fish."

"I don't want to fish."

"You want me to bring some fish up? Maybe you could trade with someone down-country."

"I don't want any of their damn fish either. What the hell do I have to trade? Dirty laundry? Golf clubs?"

There was no helping someone like that, Teri had decided. Still, she had worried about them. The children were young, just four and seven years old. Camille had trained them well; they could do the laundry with just a little bit of help, but the water splashed all over and Ralph went wild if he had to clean up after them. The older boy was able to help prepare food, but the four-year-old, disgruntled by his mother's absence, got more ornery every day. He cried, fought about getting dressed, fought about getting undressed. Ralph finally let him spend the day naked. Ralph had never thought much of his wife's religion, but now, once he found out that his daughter had died, now that his wife left him alone with the kids, now he was disgusted.

No one knew whether Ralph planned the whole thing, whether he got the idea during the meeting, or if he just lost control in the struggle to get the kids to bed that night. He took the gun and shot both the children and then himself. Alex, the neighbor who'd given him the gun, found their bodies the next day when he'd gone over to double-check whether Ralph knew how to handle a revolver or not.

The night after Bea told Teri what had happened, Koken had held her while she wept. Koken didn't know what to say. "Don't think about it," he murmured.

But it wasn't until Teri was telling Mike the story that she started wondering: how did Bea know about this if she hadn't been up-country? She was still wondering about it as she rolled the dough for the wontons she was taking up the mountain for the Christmas party.

Teri tried to concentrate on the cooking. She had been up since early morning, when it was still completely dark, to prepare the food. She was using the last of their wheat flour to make fried wontons. She rolled the dough very thin so the flour would go further. She felt sick to think this was the last, but the wontons would be special. She wanted to make something special.

Koken was tinkering with the lighting mechanism for the tower. Already he and some of his old buddies from the shop had erected the structure on Pali Beach. The tower stood almost ten feet tall on the Pali, and it was strong enough to withstand the wind. Koken was very proud, but he didn't talk to Teri about it. Ever since she'd heard about Ralph, she'd had no heart for talking.

They would have to leave in early afternoon to make it up-country before late evening. That meant walking through the cane fields in the worst heat of the day. Still, Teri was excited. She knew things were better up by Lono, not so much sickness. She would be leaving the smell of it behind her, and she was anxious to see Jan again.

"You almost ready there?" Koken put his head into the kitchen.

"Here, you could help me," Teri replied. Her fingers were shaping the wontons like small white birds and she pointed to the bowl of dough. "You think you could roll that out while I shape them?"

They both looked down on Koken's hands, black with old grease. His neck sunk into his shoulders like a guilty child. He smiled.

"Well, maybe you could wash your hands first," Teri smiled back.

"I already have," he said. They looked at each other and laughed. It wasn't the thick, growling laugh they had heard between them since April, but rather a clear laugh they hadn't heard in months. Koken took her by the shoulders. The tension between them broke and tears fell down her face as their laughter grew louder. He held her close until the room was hushed.

"Try washing them again," Teri said, moving out of the embrace. "There's some old scouring powder in the cupboard under the sink. That might do it."

Koken sauntered over to the sink. He wanted to breathe the air Teri breathed, to be close to her. He wished he knew how to talk better so he could tell her just what he was thinking, tell her how well the radio and light signals were coming together. He scoured his hands until the only black that was left was deep in the lines around his knuckles and cuticles. Then, moving next to Teri, he took the rolling pin and gingerly patted the dough, rolling it unevenly. It tore when he tried to lift it. Teri fussed, repaired the rips, and patted it back together gently, her fingers gracefully reshaping and pinching it into perfect shapes.

In an hour the cooking was done and they dressed to go. The food they were taking up-country was carefully packed in a straw bag. They stepped out into the heat of the day, Koken walking just a bit ahead of Teri. They never held hands outside, not when someone might see them.

From her bed Jan had prepared everything. The layette set was finished, with little bits of lace and cotton ready to cradle the newborn's scrawny limbs, and bonnets to frame the round face that would stare out at the new world. Jan remembered new babies' faces as curiously old and wise, as if they retained some of the knowledge from another life, only to forget before they could speak. Everything was ready. The boys had polished the cradle. New sheets, scrubbed blankets, and sewn diapers were collected and stacked in clean white piles. Everything was perfect.

Toward the end of her last pregnancy Jan had realized that if people always lived as though they were nine months pregnant, they wouldn't think life was too short. The last month always dragged on, a tired body suddenly seeming old and stretched to its limits, beyond its limits, going along simply because it had to go on for one more month. But with this pregnancy Jan felt different. She enjoyed the moments that hung about her in the bed, that seemed to breathe like living things that might always live, changing only slightly from one hour to next, one generation to the next generation of light and shadows. Had she not occasionally been swept with a sense of loneliness, she thought she might be happy if the month went on forever.

And as she looked down the mountain, unaware of the transformation in Mahele, the town looked like a child's toy village to Jan. News of the epidemic had been kept from her; Bea and Teri were busy, that was all. Yes, Camille's congregation had returned from their adventure; it had been a bit of a debacle, but not to worry. She accepted bits of information and half lies without probing, but Camille's words still rang in her ears. When she whispered the words again to herself the baby turned in her belly. Instinctively her hands caressed the swell, calming the baby.

Christmas was coming. She had knitted the boys sweaters and slippers from the wool she'd received in a trade for some socks and a vest she'd made. It was Christmas, and this evening there was the party at Alex and Charlotte's house.

Jan was stepping out, testing her legs to see if they'd still hold her, and pressing her luck, she told the boys. She stood in front of the mirror, looking over the bottles of face cream, lipsticks, colors of eye shadow that were like the warm insides of sea shells. She touched them, limited magic. Her eyes glazed over. Apply sparingly, she thought. There won't be more when these run out. Don't cry; the mascara will smear. They are so beautiful, so beautiful, these colors.

It used to be that Jan would go through the morning ritual of putting on her make-up in ten minutes, three efficient layers. Face cream and foundation, blush, eyebrow pencil. Then her eyes, the time to experiment and play. Choose a color. Try to blend them together, a pale rainbow some mornings, another morning like a sex goddess with deep set eyes for an otherwise boring day.

This evening she had been in front of the mirror no less than twenty minutes and had hardly begun. It was the first time in months that she had brought out the small bottles and she felt awkward, like a young child with her mother's stash of creams. What the hell, she thought, it will be dark anyway. She splashed color on.

The party was Jan's first outing since September. She had prepared for it all day, trying to get the wrinkles out of her dress with a damp cloth, washing her hair in the basin, the boys bringing her several pitchers of water before she had all the suds out. And then setting her hair, and resting. She wasn't used to moving about so much. Now the boys were in their room playing with plastic space monsters. She watched them them as she passed by their door. They would put themselves to bed tonight. Michael was waiting. She ducked back into the bedroom to touch up her lipstick.

Jan was wearing a maternity dress Michael had given her when she was pregnant with Tomi. It was a rich, green jersey, not at all like the frumpy muumuus other women on the island wore, pregnant or not. She hated the standard maternity fare, peterpan collars and gingham, sometimes with bows. She didn't want to look like a teenager; she wanted to be sexy, or failing that, sophisticated. She loved the green jersey.

Jan caught herself: sophisticated, worldly. To be worldly, she mused, what was worldly now? Ulcered skin? The light-headed sensation made her stop. Don't get into it, she warned herself. Don't be morbid. It's a Christmas party. The game. Lipstick. Blue eyeshadow. Green jersey. White wine. Michael's waiting.

As she turned away from the dresser top of colors, she thought she saw Camille through the window. Of course, Jan thought, it is an illusion. Now and then she imagined she glimpsed Camille's yellow eyes staring at her, worshipping her or accusing her. Each time it made Jan grow cold.

"Honey," Michael said, poking his head through the door and pausing at the sight of his wife. He thinks I'm beautiful, Jan thought.

Michael was glad he had decided not to attend the meeting that was being held before the party. He had waited so that he could take Jan to the party himself. He wanted to tell her something. He had put it off too long. He wanted to warn her that things were different; things were not what she thought anymore.

"I'm almost ready," she told him.

"You look wonderful."

Jan, flattered and embarrassed, asked him to say good-night to the boys so they could be off. He went to check on them, and she stood again in the doorway watching her sons banter with their father about the toys, and about bedtime.

"I'm not feeling so good, Daddy," Tomi complained.

"Well, go to bed early."

"We'll be okay, Dad." Steven spoke with authority.

Jan told Tomi that there was a bit of cold herb tea in the pot for him if he had a stomach ache. There was some honey too, if he wanted to put some in the tea. She started to fuss and Steven rolled his eyes. "We'll be fine, Mom. Don't worry."

Michael stepped out of their room and put his arm around her. He looked wonderful too, she realized, dressed in pants and a tailored shirt that hadn't fit him since two years after they were married. Over the last few months he'd lost the thirty pounds gained in their thirteen years of marriage, or was it fourteen years? Jan remembered what her mother had said: once you have children, days pass like years and years pass like days. It was a long time ago. The two left together, like excited lovers, pregnant with sex.

18

Alex and Charlotte's house was filled with people when Jan and Michael arrived at the party. The meeting was already over, there had been nothing to say once they'd aired accusations that Dr. Bea had taken unnecessary risks on behalf of the congregation and she had rebutted them. Most of the guests had been drinking for a couple of hours already. The candlelight made their eyes look hollow. Half-full glasses of homebrew lay about. A friendly sot was using them as chimes and a group had gathered around him singing Christmas carols to his accompaniment. Their laughing was loud. Most of the faces were flush from drinking, and some that had been flush before were now becoming ashen and haggard from too much drink.

As Jan and Michael entered the room the voices hushed. Silent eyes fell on Jan's rounded abdomen. She wanted to hide, shocked at the look of her neighbors, embarrassed by their stares. Mustering up the voice to greet her hosts, only a weak "Merry Christmas" came from her lips. She hardly recognized the voice.

Teri hurried over to the door and hugged her. "Merry Christmas, Jan. You look wonderful. I've missed you so. Here, let me get you a glass of wine." She started over to the table where the wine bottles stood, but turned back, awkward. "Oh, let me get you a chair. Oh, no. The couch would be better. Hey, excuse me, sir, let Jan sit down there next to you," she said as she guided Jan to the couch. "I'll bring you a glass of wine."

"I'm quite all right, Teri," Jan managed a small laugh, blushed and looked desperately back at Michael who joined her on the couch. The two of them were the only ones who had dressed up. She grumbled at him, under her breath, "I thought you said this was going to be a party."

"It is," he said.

A few other guests shouted greetings at her, lifting their wine glasses, but then immediately resumed their conversations.

"Michael, go visit with the others," Jan told him. "I'm okay here." She didn't feel okay; she felt estranged from these people, these neighbors who wouldn't meet her eyes. "What is with everyone?" she whispered to him.

"It's been some time since you've been out," Michael offered weakly. He felt relieved when Teri walked back with some wine. He knew Jan had missed Teri; they could talk.

"Well, how's it going? You look so great," Teri said. Great. The muscles in Teri's face quivered at the sight of a radiantly healthy pregnant woman. She absorbed something from the women she cared for and it had been too long since she'd seen the likes of Jan. Teri knew that she herself wasn't faring well through the epidemic. She was trying to assist Bea in any way she could but there was little she could do other than cook, now that all the pregnant women had lost their babies, everyone except Jan. Cooking soup and stews occupied most of her days, and even if Koken helped her sometimes, catching the fish for the stews, occasionally delivering the meals to the hospital, there was no energy left between them. In another year, Teri thought, maybe it will be different. Koken just mumbled when she'd said so.

"I guess I should wish you a merry Christmas," Jan said.

Teri sat down next to Jan as her confidant and protector. "I'm so glad you decided to come. You do look terrific, really. How does it feel to be out of the house?"

"Great."

"You add dimension to the party," Teri smiled, patting Jan's belly.

"I feel a bit awkward, huge really." Jan leaned over and whispered to Teri, "Why is everyone acting so odd? I feel like a spectacle."

"You are. It's beautiful."

"Well, they don't make me feel beautiful. Let's talk about something else. How is everything going for you?"

Teri looked at her, trying to figure how much Jan knew. "Sorry I haven't been up for awhile. There's so much to do. You know, the Christmas rush!" Teri laughed. "Actually, we are getting a big Christmas feast together for some people down-country, the people in the hospital." She didn't see the look of comprehension she'd been searching for in Jan's face.

"We'll be using some of the taro and making laulau. Can you believe it?" Teri continued, covering up the other truths in the victory of the taro project. "We're finally harvesting some taro leaves, even if we won't have a whole crop of tubers until March."

"It's really an accomplishment," Jan congratulated Teri. "And how people mocked us when we started it!"

"They're still laughing. At least Koken is laughing at me. But he'll eat the poi. You can bet on that. They're getting plenty sick of the food they've been scavenging on the beach. Now they agree that sooner or later we'll need some regular staples. And it looks like we'll have some sooner than they thought. You've heard? We're growing rice now, too."

"The boys told me," Jan nodded. "Oh, thanks for letting them help you. They seem to enjoy taking care of the little kids. At least that's all they talk about."

Teri stared into Jan's calm eyes and tried to slow her own thoughts down. She needed to be able to chat, to chat like old times, to chat about Steven and Tomi, how grown up Steven was getting, and how much help he'd been, but Teri hadn't been to the paddies since the epidemic broke out. She continued chattering.

"Steven sure is good with the little ones. He's given them pointers on archery. He's forming them into his own little army," she laughed, searched Jan's face for alarm. How much did the boys tell her? Did they tell her about the contaminated reservoir? There were no wrinkles around Jan's eyes, no concern was creasing her translucent skin. Word had gotten out down-country; she had heard about it, but apparently Jan knew nothing about the hot spot, the poisoned dust that had collected in the run off and had pooled in the old pond.

"Did they show you those bows and arrows they've been making?" Teri asked. This was safe. "I was given one as a present. The children whittle down sticks to make points and Steven made some bows out of green wood. The kids spend hours learning to shoot with him in the paddies. It keeps them busy. They adore Steven."

Jan was proud of her sons when she listened to Teri. Across the room the men were exchanging hunting stories, and Jan just caught words, here and there. A year ago these men had been busy in different occupations, broken into classes they'd protected with language and manners. Now they were all scavengers, hunters and farmers on their small plots of land and backyard gardens, but their talk was only about hunting.

Bea was there in a linen skirt that looked worn and greasy. She'd spoken at the meeting about the precautions they could take to prevent the spread of infection, and her job was done. Like Teri, she was glad for the excuse to come up-country to Lono, away from the sick, but she hadn't anticipated the hostility these people felt towards her. Now she was getting drunk although she still maintained a strong reserve. Jan caught her eye, but Bea turned away.

"Hey, I've got to talk to Bea a minute," Teri excused herself.

"I'm stuck in this couch," Jan laughed.

"Don't move then."

"Well, come back and visit with me more."

"I'll be right back."

Jan sat by herself on the couch and surveyed the crowd. A year ago, they looked like a different group of people. Now they talked faster, looked older, many had greyed. As she sat on the couch watching the faces the baby began kicking vigorously, and then her stomach contracted. It startled her, but the sensation passed so quickly she was sure she was not going into real labour. She'd had these little contractions for a month before each of the boys' births. She patted her belly, wondering if the baby was frightened by the sudden tightening in its space. She and Michael would have to settle on names soon.

Teri joined a group of women that had gathered around Bea. The women were still grilling Bea about the risks she took getting involved with the congregation.

"You don't know what it has been like for those people. They tried to make do with nothing," Bea spat out, referring to the survivors in the congregation. She was on the defensive, furious. "They needed food. They had a right to food. We were even short of water. They choked. Some died right away, but some just kept choking, without water. It was disgusting. You would have left in a minute."

"You are such a hero, doctor. You know best. You've seen it all. Well, this is something new. If you ask me, you know about as much as the next fool. They didn't have to go over there in the first place," a young woman argued.

"Shh," Teri warned. She didn't want Jan to overhear the argument, but no one paid her any notice.

"You took another risk, doctor. We're running out of chances here. Maybe it's more information for your study, though, Bea. What's the point of arguing?" The young woman poured herself more wine, while water welled up in Bea's eyes as she tried desperately to hold back her anger, and the group of women continued staring at her.

Jan lay back on the sofa cushions and looked over the gathering, contented. Grey hair, new jobs, new foods, everything was different. These people are surviving, Jan thought, and not just because they are lucky. They are strong and they hold together. The hardness in their faces Jan counted only as a cover for their losses. A sensation swept over her that she hardly recognized as compassion. Yes, she thought, I like these people. They've been good to my family and me.

She considered her own sheltered life of the past few months. At first it had seemed like a hardship, to be bedridden, and she'd panicked, but now it had been a blessing for Jan, a chance to think things over, to hide. In many ways she'd lived as if there hadn't been any changes. Her condition had been a protective blanket she'd pulled over her whole body. No one else had been so lucky. But these people had kept her safe, and fed her family, and so she loved them now.

Jan caught Teri's eye. Teri was staring at her, looking furtive and protective. Jan smiled. Teri's face relaxed. Teri is a little kitchen witch, Jan thought. So tiny and old-looking now. There's a wise woman look about her.

Alex, who was hosting the party, glanced over to the women talking in the corner, noticing the angry grimace. "A little tiff among the hens in the chicken coop?" he slurred, half drunk.

"Shut up," Charlotte snapped.

"Honey, this is our Christmas party. Where's the Christmas cheer? Come on, women. It's time for carols." Alex called over to the men. "Come on everyone. It's song time."

Charlotte offered Bea a weak, reconciling smile. "Look, I'm sorry. Let's sing and forget about it tonight."

"Sure," Bea nodded.

They gathered around the wine glass chimes. The musician took up his fork and tried to hit a note on a half empty glass. "Is that high C?"

"Go on," some people chided, the man began clinking out a tune, and they started a round of 'Deck the Halls'.

Michael walked over to Jan. "Can I bring you a chair over there so you can join us?"

"Honey, I think we should go soon," Jan said.

"After a few carols." He helped her up and they moved toward the group. She felt cumbersome. The wine had made her tired. The carols were making her homesick.

"We three kings from orient are, bearing gifts we travel so far. Hills and fountains, moors and mountains, following yonder star"; "Here comes Santa Claus, here somes Santa Claus, right down Santa Claus Lane"; "Oh Christmas tree, oh Christmas tree, your leaves for e'er delight us". Song after song, everyone was drinking more and hitting fewer notes, and no one heard the knock at the door except Jan. She tugged at Michael's arm. "Should I get it?"

"What?"

"The door. Someone's at the door."

"I'll get it." Michael crossed the room with his drink in his hand. He threw open the door to welcome the latecomer. A soldier stood there, dressed in what must have been his last clean uniform. A rifle rested against his thigh, and without saying a word the soldier grabbed it up and stepped into the hallway. All the eyes of the group fell on him and the music stopped abruptly.

Jan recognized him. He was the man who had come to do the census. She blushed and looked down at her belly, hoping he wouldn't recognize her now, but he stared right at her.

"I need to talk to a few of you, privately," the soldier said. "One at a time, starting with you, lady." He nodded to Jan.

Alex, drunk as he was, still thought he could take charge, it being his house. He came over to the soldier and sneered. "You are interrupting our party, mister. What did you say your name was?"

The soldier looked stony-eyed. "My name is Corporal Jack Thomas, and I am sorry about your party, but I have to talk to the lady. It will only take a minute, sir."

"Your timing is lousy, soldier."

"I'll speak to the man," Koken said, moving out from the corner of the room. "One minute won't ruin my evening."

"I'll want to talk with you too, later, mister, but I have to talk to the lady with the baby first. She's had visitors, and they've told her more than she's saying."

All eyes in the room rested on Jan, and she was filled with confusion. What was he talking about? Visitors? The people who'd been bringing her mending? Camille?

"Koken, let me speak with him," Teri said. She stepped in front of her husband. "Why don't we step into the bedroom, sir?" She picked up her handbag as she passed a stack of shoes and bags in the hall.

"Hey, Jack," Bea called to him across the room. "How are you?" She sidled up close to him as the others watched. Now Jack's face filled with confusion.

"Oh, hello, doctor. I didn't expect to find you here. Do you know these people?" he mumbled.

"Why, of course I do. They're dear old friends of mine. We thought we should get together for Christmas. I'm so glad you could join us."

"I'm here on business, ma'am."

"Oh, nonsense. It's Christmas. Have a drink."

"No, thank you, ma'am. I need to talk to the pregnant lady."

"Oh, you don't want to be bothering her. Let's you and me just step back here and see if I can help you." Bea looked at Teri out of the corner of her eye, and Teri passed her the handbag. With her free hand, Bea picked up a candle stick to light her way down the hall. "Just step this way, Jack. I think there's a quiet room back this way where we can talk. Are you sure I can't get you a drink, though?" she said.

"No, thank you, ma'am."

The rest of the group stared at Bea and the soldier as they disappeared down the hallway.

"Where were we? Who can start us on 'Joy To The World'," Teri said, but no one responded. "Sing," she hissed. The music began.

"...Let heaven and nature sing. Let heaven and nature sing. Let heaven and nature, and nature..." A gunshot blasted out from the bedroom. "Dr. Bea!" Koken shouted and ran to the bedroom door.

"She's okay," Teri shouted after him.

Bea met him at the doorway. The group saw Koken peer into the bedroom. "One more down," he muttered.

"Oh Christ," Michael said, shaking his head. "Here?"

"He was going crazy," Bea shook her head. "There's only the two of them left. He said he just wanted to do his job; he wanted to take Jan to the hospital."

"What are you talking about?"

"His job," Bea repeated. "Rounding up those who have been exposed. The quarantine." Bea spoke in a monotone. "They knew what was going on, but he wasn't interested in getting even."

"What? What's going on?" Charlotte demanded.

Michael put up his hand to Koken and Teri. "Come on over here. Let's everyone sit down.".

"Sit down? A man is dying in my bedroom!" Charlotte shouted.

"It's too late for first aid, dear," Alex mumbled.

"He's already dead," Bea said.

Charlotte stared at her. "Well, that's just fine. Are you going to just leave him there?"

"No, we'll bury him," Koken said.

"Well, isn't that nice," Charlotte shook her head.

Jan felt herself pull back from the group. Her hands covered most of her face but her fingers opened to take in the whole gathering. She could hardly believe it; no one else was shocked. A man had been shot in the next room, but no one was shocked.

Michael tried to be heard above the chattering. "Okay. Let's just everyone calm down. Koken, why don't you and I take the body down to the ditch and put a bit of dirt over it? We can bury it properly in the morning."

Jan stared at her husband. He was talking, but now it was as if he were a stranger, casually directing traffic. She couldn't believe it. A drunk guest hollered, "Would someone like to tell us what's going on?"

"Dr. Bea just shot a soldier in my bedroom," Charlotte said. "It's disgusting."

"I didn't get anything messy. I was careful," Bea said, her speech slurred.

"And it's probably best we don't discuss this any more," said Koken. He walked over to Michael and spoke softly, but Jan overheard every word. "Look, there's only one soldier left on this island and he's going to go crazy, Michael, when he finds out that his buddy is gone."

Michael looked over at Dr. Bea, and nodded toward Koken. Bea handed Koken the gun. Jan looked at Teri, but didn't catch her eye. Teri stared at her husband, knowingly and sadly.

"So I can assume you guys have been knocking these soldiers off, one by one," Bea stared at Koken and Michael and then shrugged. "I didn't know."

"Dr. Bea," Alex said to her. "These soldiers were sent to this island when it looked like a war was going to break out, for God knows what reason. Does it make sense to you that they'd come here to fight a war? They were either so stupid they were dangerous to the army, or else they had some job to do. Besides, we didn't start this."

"Yeah, it was some guys down in Mahele started the shooting. Not us," Koken said. "We didn't shoot until there was a real threat."

"Yeah? Like this guy, coming to get Jan? Fine." Bea shrugged her shoulders and shook her head.

"You did the right thing, Dr. Bea. We were right to be afraid of them," Alex said. "Just sorry it had to be you to do the job. They thought they were in charge. It goes to a guy's head. You go a little crazy. We all did." He looked around to see some heads nodding agreement. "To be tops if you're a soldier is to rout out the enemy. Those guys were making enemies out of all of us."

"It seems they would have hit the mark right on there," Bea said and turned away from the group.

Jan could feel the trembling begin again in her whole body. They were talking about fifteen, maybe twenty, murders. The trembling became worse. She started gagging.

"Oh God," Teri called, seeing Jan across the room.

Michael hurried next to her. "Here, honey, lie down on the couch here," he said, trying to guide her over to the sofa. She shrank from his hands. He didn't seem to notice.

Teri hurried over to her and put a pillow under her head as Michael laid Jan down. Jan looked straight at Teri. Had Teri known about this all along? Jan wondered. Her stomach wrenched. Teri looked impassive as she took Jan's pulse.

Michael leaned over toward Koken and whispered to him, "I mean it, Koken. The last one's going to go nuts when he figures out that his buddy is gone."

"I'll take care of it," Koken said. He signalled to another man and the two of them slipped into the bedroom. The others gathered around Jan, and she stared up at their lined faces. They looked very far away. No one took much notice as the two men left with the soldier's body wrapped in a bed sheet. A large, red spot of blood was all that distinguished their bundle from so much laundry.

"We've got to get her home to bed," Jan heard Teri say to Michael. The two of them lifted her into Michael's arms. Jan could barely feel their arms as they strained to lift her. She stared up at the stars while they carried her down the street. Halfway to their home Koken joined them. Jan heard his voice tell Teri that she had better spend the night at Jan's. Jan knew for certain, then, that Koken was appointed to kill the last soldier, and she sensed Teri's tacit agreement. The stars were the only things she saw clearly.

In the house Michael lit the way to the bedroom with candles. Teri helped Jan out of her dress and put her into bed as Michael went in to check on the boys. Jan was too weak to pull away from Teri's hands. The two women said nothing to each other. Jan curled up into the bed and pulled the comforters over her body. She heard Michael call Teri into the hall as she fell into a deep sleep.

19

In the hall Teri saw that Michael was panic-stricken. "The boys," he whispered. "They're covered with vomit. Both of them. They are almost unconscious." She ran down the hall with Michael to the children's bedroom, but before she entered the room she could smell the vomit and diarrhea. She stopped, stepped in slowly and stared at the two boys, lying in their beds, covered by dirty white sheets. She walked over to Tomi's bed, put her hand to his forehead and felt the fever warming her palm immediately. Steven was muttering unintelligibly in his sleep. She signalled Michael to come with her, back into the hall, where she leaned against the wall, unable to hold up her own weight. She stared at Michael. He looked at her and then shot his eyes back into the bedroom to look at his two sons. He stared at Teri as she began talking.

"Your boys found the children playing in the old reservoir," she mumbled. "It was too late by the time we found out."

Michael looked at her, comprehending nothing. "What are you saying?"

Teri's lips moved, but there was no sound.

Michael's eyes widened until they seemed to break open with water and his cry seemed to come from somewhere deep in the mountain itself. Teri stretched her hands out to place them on his shoulder, but her own mind raced back to the taro paddies, counting the number of children who had always come with their mothers, counting the number of children who must have been there the day Steven found them in the reservoir, playing as if it were a pond in the Garden of Eden.

She didn't say anything more. In time Michael's groans quieted, and, when Teri pulled herself away from the wall to begin washing the children, Michael followed her. The two of them went into the bathroom, filled a basin with water and soap, took towels into the boys' room and sponged the boys' bodies down. They cleaned up the vomit, changed the children's sheets, and made cold compresses for their faces. Occasionally they would look in on Jan to make sure she was still sleeping. Jan rested fitfully, sleep holding her mercifully through the night.

Toward midnight the boys' fevers rose. Teri knew Bea should be called, and wondered if she could get a message to her with the flashing lights. Bea wouldn't have travelled far down the mountain at this hour, a few miles at the most. She must be staying at someone's home until morning. Teri could get a message to her at any home along the network, but neither she nor Michael knew the code. She flashed a flashlight spasmodically, hoping there was a receiver who would recognize trouble. Bea must be staying at someone's home until morning.

The boys were slipping into a coma, unable to take the tea Teri spooned into their slack mouths. The fever wasn't subsiding. Michael continued sponging their bodies, his motions becoming mechanical and his face rigid while his body curled over his sons. The silence had a hold on him again.

Teri hurried to the window to try flashing light signals once more. This time lights flickered an answer she could not interpret, but she saw a message being passed on down the mountain. It occurred to her that Bea might not have even left the party. Teri couldn't wait any longer and ran out of the house, down the street to find her.

By the time she arrived at Alex and Charlotte's house, she was too breathless to speak. Alex, who had answered the door, grinned and swept his arms out from his sides, beckoning Teri to come inside. Teri saw that people were still drinking, several sitting, slumped on chairs and the sofa. "Is the baby coming?" another man asked, sounding both hopeful and afraid.

"No. Quick. Get Dr. Bea," Teri said, and then lowered her voice. "It's the boys. They're dying."

Bea heard Teri's words from the bedroom where she'd been resting. She dressed and came into the hallway, exchanging a look with Teri that was full of the knowledge they held in common. The resignation came into Teri's body and her head sank down on her bowed neck. Bea led Teri out of the house and back down the street. Teri had caught her breath as they walked and slowly, blankly, she described what she'd found at the house. Bea showed no emotion either, but moved quickly to keep up with Teri. "How about Jan?" she queried.

"Asleep. She knows nothing about it."

As they reached the house Teri's eyes squeezed shut and she jerked to a standstill, suddenly frozen. Bea looked around them, to see what had frightened Teri, but there was nothing to see. Teri's face was blank when Bea peered into it, her own brow knitted. "Teri?" she called to her gently. Teri didn't respond; she saw and heard nothing. Bea took her hand and opened the door. Teri's legs moved stiffly before a shiver ran through her body and her muscles relaxed. "Let's go," she said.

They crept into the boys' room. Michael moved out of the way to give Bea room to make her cursory examination. "Have you tried to get them to take any liquids?" Bea asked Teri.

Teri nodded. "They couldn't take anything."

Michael studied the women's faces. He found, on their faces, the news that his two boys were going to die.

Bea had seen the symptoms so often lately, the sudden nausea that became worse till nothing could relieve it. The symptoms were so like those of the congregation , different more in intensity rather than in kind from the earliest fatalities last April. For children it would end quickly. She couldn't watch, not again. She lay down on the couch in the living room and, pulling her notebook out of her bag, she wrote a few notes silently. She would stay. Jan might need her later in the night.

Teri and Michael held the two boys until the sun reddened the sky.

December 22

So I killed the last soldier.

It wasn't me, but rather fear.

It was me possessed by everything around me, taking over my body while I observed everything.

No. It was me. I killed a man. His name was Jack.
Both Tomi and Steven have had it.

20

Having buried the soldier, Koken had one more job to do before going home. It took him almost until morning to make his way down the mountain, with the gun Alex gave him tucked in the jacket slung over his shoulder. During the long walk Koken didn't think about anything at all. Instead he took in the shadowy scene at the base of the mountain. In the cane fields he heard mongoose scurrying in and around the stalks. Their beady eyes studied him as he passed.

When he reached the barracks in Mahele he slid in behind some nearby bushes and listened for the sound that would tell him that the last soldier was up and around. There was no such sound. Taking his gun from his jacket pocket he crept over to a window, slowly lifted himself up to the sill and peered in. It took his eyes a moment to adjust before he could see the dark shadows in the room, the forms of the desk and cots. Nothing moved in the large dorm, and the only light was the moonlight streaming in over Koken's shoulder.

Finally he caught sight of the soldier slumped over a chair. He lifted the gun to shoot at the first sign of movement, but there was none. Something about the way the man's head was crooked, bent over toward the bed at an impossible angle, told Koken he had no need to use a bullet. The soldier was already dead.

Koken didn't want to investigate. If the soldier had been killed, then whoever had done it might still be lurking about. If the soldier had been suddenly taken by an illness, Koken didn't want to be exposed to it. Probably no one would ever want to use the barracks again so there was no need to bury the body; the building itself could be the man's tomb. Koken crept along the outside wall and moved toward the front door that had been left ajar, watching for any movement in the bushes beyond the yard. He slipped his hand around to the inside of the lock and released the catch, so when he slammed the door shut, it was locked from the inside. The slam was frighteningly loud in the absolute silence of the night, but still there was no movement in the bushes. Koken straighted up, returned the

153

gun to his jacket pocket, and walked the rest of the distance home.

Koken thought of Teri spending the night at Jan's, supervising her care. He'd been through it with her before, her protective ways once a woman was near her time to deliver. Teri entered the pregnant woman's own space, and couldn't be budged. If Jan didn't need her at the house he knew Teri would sleep over at a neighbor's just to be closer, just in case. At his front door he looked up the mountain and caught the last flickered light of a message that was being sent down and flashed to a house toward the base of the mountain. Someone was sick, or perhaps Jan was in labour. He couldn't make out the signal.

He went into the house and lit a candle by the radio. Only a few more wires needed to be soldered. He caressed the casing of the large lamp that would send its beam across the water. Tomorrow he was going to finish the soldering and double-check all the mechanisms. Then he would load the machine into his cart and pull it across the island to the Pali Beach. It might take several days to set it all up. He wanted to stay there long enought to make sure that was no problem with the transmitter. He'd leave a note for Teri. It was better that she was gone. This way they wouldn't have to get into another argument and go over it all again.

For three days the boys lay in bed, barely conscious. When Jan awoke, and discovered that her children were stricken, she entered into Michael's silence where neither Bea nor Teri could reach her. Bea and Teri stayed at the house all the while looking after the family. Bea made a few trips back to the neighbors' house. She came up with a bottle of old whisky to give the boys some relief from their pain if they ever came around enough to need it. Liquor was the only pain-killer available, scarce as it was, and Bea was glad to have it, if not for the boys then for Jan.

News of the latest victims spread up and down the mountain. A neighbor whispered to Bea when she came over to the house with a pot of soup; two more children were stricken down-country. Being younger they died quickly. Bea said nothing about these deaths to either Jan or Teri.

Teri had entered into her own hidden place. As she sat on the edge of Tomi's bed, she remembered the boys' visits in her home when they were quite little. Tomi was just a few months old the first time Jan left them with her for her to baby-sit. He was a wizened little bundle, lying quiet and content as his older brother raced through the house, confused and angry whenever Tomi cried, wanting it all to be like it used to be. Teri was patient with Steven and her patience healed his hurt. They would rock Tomi back to sleep so they could read stories together and play with the little bears and Steven's stuffed lion. Years had passed like that. They had both grown into fine boys. Teri had noticed Steven's patience as he entertained the young children in the taro paddies. They had grown strong and tall, both of them, but now they lay shrunken and looked so small, there between the sheets.

When she and Koken were young they had wanted children of their own, just like Jan's children, to fill their home with noise and work and games. Teri would offer the children back to Jan at the end of each visit, glad to have shared their play for awhile. Now, as Michael and Jan came into the room, she offered them back again, moving out of the room so the two parents could be alone with their children.

Jan mumbled prayers, occasionally singing quiet songs to her sons. Steven gained some strength as the second day wore on. Michael spoke not at all. Sometimes he got up to carry in fresh water, on the third day he went out briefly to feed the livestock. But most of the days he just sat by the boys' beds and stared.

Bea had no heart for any of it. She did her job—did whatever she could—taking a pulse, checking a heart-beat, then moved out of the room again. Oddly, it was the neighbors in Lono who gave Bea refuge, taking her into their homes, burying their anger. They fed her, offered her clean clothes, and sent her back to the house with dishes of fried rice or pots of fish soup. They spoke little to each other. Bea would give brief accounts of the boys' deterioration, or say how Jan was doing, but each report was the same. The boys were going down slowly. Jan was holding up, silent, numb.

On the third day, when Michael and Bea had both stepped out, Jan called Teri into the boys' bedroom. She had been sitting up with her sons for several hours despite Bea's protests that she must lie down, if just for an hour. But she couldn't leave them, couldn't let them out of her sight for even a moment. Bea had finally given up coaxing her and gone out to pick up more food. Occasionally Jan held one of the boys in her arms, but mostly she just stared impassively. Now when she called, Teri came running.

"Teri, I want to baptize them," Jan told her.

Teri had to strain to hear the mumbled words. "Should I get someone? A priest?" she asked.

"There's no time, and who would come? I'll do it if I can remember how," Jan replied.

"Maybe we should wait for Michael? Should I go try and find him?"

Jan looked at Teri and shook her head. Michael would remain silent. It was no use including him. "They have to be baptized," Jan said, and then her body trembled, swept with panic. "But Teri, I don't remember the words. Do you think it will be okay if I just did it myself? Made up some words? Say yes."

Teri wanted to cry, seeing this strong woman so suppliant. "Jan, I don't know. I don't know about these things, but I'm sure it would be okay."

"I need a bowl of water and some oil," Jan said, straightening up.

Teri ran and got her the water, some oil, and a towel. When she got back Jan had smoothed out the boys' bedclothes. She had folded their hands on their chests which heaved occasionally, but did not bring in the breath that could return them to consciousness. Jan had removed most of her own clothing, and stood there almost naked, bulging with child. Tears flooded Teri's eyes when she saw Jan.

Jan turned to her and stated, matter-of-factly, "I'm going to baptize the new one as well. I'm afraid for it, Teri. Do you have the things?" Teri passed them to her. "I wish I had a Bible," Jan muttered. "But I think I can remember."

She took the bowl and made a sign of the cross over the water. "God, forgive me if I make a mistake. God, accept my children. Forgive me. Forgive us all." Jan's tears mixed with the water as she dripped it gingerly over Steven's forehead. "Steven, I baptize you in the name of your creator, the child of God, and the Spirit."

She turned again to Teri, who looked frightened. "Is that right?" Jan asked. "Oh God, I have to do it right and I don't know the words."

Teri stared at the foreign ritual, an ancient ceremony she barely understood. Jan repeated the words, dripping the water over Tomi's forehead. Then she poured oil into her hands and rubbed it in her palm to warm it. She muttered words Teri couldn't hear, massaged the oil on the children's lips, on the palms of their hands and on the soles of their cold blue feet, finally making the sign of the cross with the oil on their foreheads. From within the coma Steven's lips moved, speaking words that took no shape, that were not audible.

After baptizing the boys Jan sat at the edge of Steven's bed. Her face was wet from tears but set like stone, her tears were like rain sliding down a rock, and she was seeing nothing anymore. She began pouring the water over her distended belly, again mumbling words, and then rubbing the oil over the taut skin.

Teri suppressed a horrified laugh. Jan looked to her like a goddess calling to her lover, her breasts drooping over the ivory mound of her abdomen.

"God, forgive me," Teri whispered to herself. "Accept our children."

When Bea and Michael returned, they found the two women standing there over the children, Jan still undressed with her hands resting on her naked abdomen, Teri leaning, silent, against the wall. Michael sat down next to Jan, draping a blanket over her and holding her rigid body. Eventually Jan stood up and pulled her robe around herself. "I'll get us some lunch," she said, her lips barely moving. Teri began to protest, but Bea put her finger to her own lips, signalling Teri to let Jan be. Jan gathered herself together and moved into the kitchen. The others remained in the boys' room. They listened to the pots banging, as Jan built up the fire and poured water into a kettle to boil. A few minutes later she came into the bedroom with four bowls of broth that she gave to each adult. Sitting down on Tomi's bed she tried to spoon some broth from her own bowl into his mouth. Bea and Teri quietly moved out of the room, leaving Jan and Michael alone with their sons.

After a few hours both the boys were dead.

As twilight entered the room, turning it a warm pink, Jan stood up, dressed herself, went out into the back yard and walked toward the gully. Michael, Bea, and Teri followed her, watching her pick up the garden shovel that she had traded her canned fruit to get. She began to dig. She ignored their protests and went on digging. After ten minutes Michael took the shovel from her and continued the job. They took turns digging, saying nothing.

That evening they brought their children's bodies out, laying them on white sheets at the bottom of the pit in the light of the moon. Not having the heart to cover the bodies with dirt, they returned to the house in silence. Teri stayed behind to fill in the grave.

21

All night Michael watched Jan moan and toss in her sleep. He didn't touch her. Their separate pain put such a distance between them, they were like two mountain ridges with black water running through the gully between them breaking rock. After a time Jan's groans became louder. Still, she remained unconscious.

Michael finally went to Teri who was sleeping on the couch in the living room. Shaking her shoulder, he nodded his head. "It's now."

Teri's sleep had been light, and she took in the meaning of Michael's words immediately. "How is she?" she asked, pushing her hair off her face. Michael didn't answer. He led Teri into the bedroom.

The room was very dark. Only the faint light of the moon through the window outlined Jan's body, and the tightening of her belly was barely visible beneath the thin cotton nightgown. Teri and Michael watched the troubled woman in silence. Occasionally, pain racked her swollen body and her face would become contorted. Still she resisted consciousness.

"Perhaps I should be timing these," Michael thought aloud. Teri weakly offered him her watch, recognizing the need he would feel to do something, anything, during the hours that lay ahead.

"I've never seen a woman sleep through her entire labour. Let's leave her be as long as we can. Sleep is merciful," Teri said. "You should try to sleep too, Michael. It might be a long day. Call me when she wakes up." Teri left him alone to continue his vigil.

In the dark Jan seemed like an old woman to Michael; an old wise woman who was dying. He stared at her body which alternately twitched and then relaxed. Time seemed to move so slowly, sometimes forward, sometimes back. Michael's mind drifted back to the first birth, Steven's birth. Jan had insisted that Michael be there though he had protested, dreading the blood, his helplessness in it. In the end he was glad he'd been there, Jan writhing and shrieking one minute, the next moment her eyes were wide with enthusiasm. "Our baby, it's coming!" Then again the wild force of the contraction. "Oh, damn. It's coming. It's coming." A black curl of hair in the opening to her vagina. Push. Push. My God, how would it get through there? A miracle. Push, now. Water and blood. My God, our baby. Steven.

Jan's eyes did not open. She slept through still another contraction, and Michael stared out the bedroom window, hoping to see morning light.

At the second birth, Michael remembered, they had confidently informed the doctor of their progress. Michael had fiddled with the watch. Six centimetres dilated. Four minutes apart. We'll call you when we need you. Thanks. No problem, Doc. A miracle. Tomi.

Gone. Michael's face was wet. Remembering made him feel hollowed out. Jan's moans echoed in the hollow space inside his chest. His babies. This grief with no name had become, for everyone on the island, like the air they breathed. It left neighbors incapable of saying "I'm sorry your children died. It must be very hard." No one would attempt to comfort him; his children were just two more buried in the rock, gone. Die in a direct hit and you're lucky, Michael thought. The hollowness is blasted out in an instant. No pain. Michael's cousins, certainly dead. Their old landlord, certainly dead. Everything one loved and hated gone in the same blast. Big bang. Expanding universe. No boundaries but limited. No name. Not Tomi or Steven.

Jan's groans became more regular, closer together. Finally her eyes opened, glazed with the pain of a contraction. Michael ran into the hall and called Teri, then crept up next to Jan to hold her hand on the bed. The sheets were soaked with her sweat. She lay in a small puddle of thick blood, arching her neck to stare at Michael. "The baby, Michael, it's coming."

"Yes." Michael was surprised to hear his own voice, calm and confident. "You're okay. Just concentrate. You'll be fine."

Jan's eyes became more glassy with the next contraction. Michael looked desperately at the door for Teri to come. "Oh, God," Jan shouted, but as the pain subsided Jan breathed deeply. "Michael. This baby is the promised one."

Michael wondered if she was delirious. He wanted to check her blood pressure, her pulse. He desperately wished he had some equipment, even just a stethoscope, something to give him facts, something that would prove she was okay, that she'd be fine.

Jan knew he didn't believe her. "Michael, it is true. Keep it in your heart. This baby is the one who is to come. All the others died, Michael. . .Oh, God..." A contraction cut off her words. She groaned loudly and grabbed at his sleeve, holding onto him and gritting her teeth. Again the pain subsided. She glared at him, condemning his skepticism. "You wait and see. Camille told me so. This is the one. God so loved the world..." Another contraction. She shrieked, then fell into a consciousness where he could not enter; focused, angry, certain.

Teri came in with Bea. Michael moved out of the way as they pulled back the sheets. Teri ran for some towels. Bea checked for dilation. The contractions came quickly, with only moments between them. Jan hardly noticed; she twitched wildly but made no noise. Teri hurried back into the living room to start up the fire and began boiling water to sterilize Bea's equipment.

"Michael, hold her!" Bea shouted at him. Like an obedient child he hurried to his wife's side. Jan crouched up into the next pain, pushing again and again. An hour passed with intermittent pain and peace. The women bustled back and forth, washing, setting out the birthing tools and getting more water.

During that hour the sky began changing slowly. The thick black gave way to indigo. Messages had been flashed up and down the mountain and the house starting filling with people, silent people with blank faces. Neighbors. No words for each other.

Teri returned to the bedroom with more wet cloths. Jan sucked on a wet rag. "What are these people doing here?" Bea hissed at Teri. Teri shrugged. "Get rid of them," Bea growled at Michael.

Helplessly Michael wandered into the hallway. Their friends stood in the doorways. The living room was crowded with neighbors. Someone put out a hand to stroke Michael's bathrobe. Camille had arrived, dirty and tattered. No one questioned her. No one would break the hush of the waiting.

At the sight of Camille, confusion overtook Michael. "You've got to go," he pleaded with the group. No one responded with any movement at all, and he wondered if the words had been audible.

Had he spoken? Did he know how to speak? He turned back to the bedroom.

"Michael, it's coming. The baby!" Teri called to him. He ran in to be next to Jan, to see the head emerging. Bea was propping up Jan's legs, waiting. "Careful, now," she said. "Don't push too soon here. Okay, slowly now. Now push!"

Teri helped Jan lift her back into the contraction. Jan squealed and clenched her teeth as she felt the stretching. She grunted.

"Push, push, push," Teri insisted. "Now, easy now." The baby's head was crowning.

"It's coming! Our baby!" Jan grasped Michael's hands.

"Again now, Jan," Teri directed her softly. "Push," and the baby's body slithered into Bea's hands. Teri handed her a warm towel and they bundled the baby into it.

Bea winced at the sight of the small shape.

"Our baby, our baby, Michael. It's our baby. Give me my baby," Jan was weeping. Michael stared at Teri's strained face.

"Jan, it's a boy," Teri whispered. Bea tipped the baby downward, trying to start its breathing. The baby remained limp and bluish.

"Why isn't it crying?" Jan panicked.

"It's okay." Teri reassured her.

Bea blew gently on the baby's face. Weakly, it gave out its first cry. Relief filled the bedroom, spreading down the hall into the living room. There was one sigh, breathed as if by the whole gathering. They closed their eyes. Some prayed with Camille. Bea gazed at the baby's eyes and whispered something almost inaudible; it sounded as if she had said Yes. Then she handed the bundle to Jan.

Jan kissed the baby, rocking and soothing him. The baby lay there, too weak to cry again. Jan was silent. She looked at the child's odd features. The back of his head swelled up into his forehead. His nose went into a lip that was cleft. Jan didn't know how to kiss him. His eyes were like slits, his ears uneven. One ear looked almost like a navel with no outer ear at all, and the stub of one arm poked out of what might have been a shoulder. His fingers wiggled at the end of the stub like tentacles, but Jan was not horrified. He looked unearthly. She held the child who was born of another world. Michael buried his face in her hair.

spoken? Did he know how to speak? He turned back to the
[roo]m.

Michael, it's coming. The baby!" Teri called to him. He ran in
next to Jan, to see the head emerging. Bea was propping up Jan's
waiting. "Careful, now," she said. "Don't push too soon here.
slowly now. Now push!"

Teri helped Jan lift her back into the contraction. Jan squealed
clenched her teeth as she felt the stretching. She grunted.
Push, push, push," Teri insisted. "Now, easy now." The baby's
was crowning.

It's coming! Our baby!" Jan grasped Michael's hands.
Again now, Jan," Teri directed her softly. "Push," and the
body slithered into Bea's hands. Teri handed her a warm
and they bundled the baby into it.

Bea winced at the sight of the small shape.
Our baby, our baby, Michael. It's our baby. Give me my
Jan was weeping. Michael stared at Teri's strained face.
Jan, it's a boy," Teri whispered. Bea tipped the baby downward,
to start its breathing. The baby remained limp and bluish.
Why isn't it crying?" Jan panicked.
It's okay." Teri reassured her.

Bea blew gently on the baby's face. Weakly, it gave out its first
relief filled the bedroom, spreading down the hall into the living
There was one sigh, breathed as if by the whole gathering.
closed their eyes. Some prayed with Camille. Bea gazed at the
eyes and whispered something almost inaudible; it sounded
she had said Yes. Then she handed the bundle to Jan.

Jan kissed the baby, rocking and soothing him. The baby lay
too weak to cry again. Jan was silent. She looked at the child's
features. The back of his head swelled up into his forehead. His
went into a lip that was cleft. Jan didn't know how to kiss him.
eyes were like slits, his ears uneven. One ear looked almost like a
with no outer ear at all, and the stub of one arm poked out of
might have been a shoulder. His fingers wiggled at the end of the
like tentacles, but Jan was not horrified. He looked unearthly.
and the child who was born of another world. Michael buried his
her hair.

21

All night Michael watched Jan moan and toss in her sleep. He didn't touch her. Their separate pain put such a distance between them, they were like two mountain ridges with black water running through the gully between them breaking rock. After a time Jan's groans became louder. Still, she remained unconscious.

Michael finally went to Teri who was sleeping on the couch in the living room. Shaking her shoulder, he nodded his head. "It's now."

Teri's sleep had been light, and she took in the meaning of Michael's words immediately. "How is she?" she asked, pushing her hair off her face. Michael didn't answer. He led Teri into the bedroom.

The room was very dark. Only the faint light of the moon through the window outlined Jan's body, and the tightening of her belly was barely visible beneath the thin cotton nightgown. Teri and Michael watched the troubled woman in silence. Occasionally, pain racked her swollen body and her face would become contorted. Still she resisted consciousness.

"Perhaps I should be timing these," Michael thought aloud. Teri weakly offered him her watch, recognizing the need he would feel to do something, anything, during the hours that lay ahead.

"I've never seen a woman sleep through her entire labour. Let's leave her be as long as we can. Sleep is merciful," Teri said. "You should try to sleep too, Michael. It might be a long day. Call me when she wakes up." Teri left him alone to continue his vigil.

In the dark Jan seemed like an old woman to Michael; an old wise woman who was dying. He stared at her body which alternately twitched and then relaxed. Time seemed to move so slowly, sometimes forward, sometimes back. Michael's mind drifted back to the first birth, Steven's birth. Jan had insisted that Michael be there though he had protested, dreading the blood, his helplessness in it. In the end he was glad he'd been there, Jan writhing and shrieking one minute, the next moment her eyes were wide with enthusiasm. "Our baby, it's coming!" Then again the wild force of the contraction. "Oh, damn. It's coming. It's coming." A black curl of hair in the opening to her vagina. Push. Push. My God, how would it get through there? A miracle. Push, now. Water and blood. My God, our baby. Steven.

Jan's eyes did not open. She slept through still another contraction, and Michael stared out the bedroom window, hoping to see morning light.

At the second birth, Michael remembered, they had confidently informed the doctor of their progress. Michael had fiddled with the watch. Six centimetres dilated. Four minutes apart. We'll call you when we need you. Thanks. No problem, Doc. A miracle. Tomi.

Gone. Michael's face was wet. Remembering made him feel hollowed out. Jan's moans echoed in the hollow space inside his chest. His babies. This grief with no name had become, for everyone on the island, like the air they breathed. It left neighbors incapable of saying "I'm sorry your children died. It must be very hard." No one would attempt to comfort him; his children were just two more buried in the rock, gone. Die in a direct hit and you're lucky, Michael thought. The hollowness is blasted out in an instant. No pain. Michael's cousins, certainly dead. Their old landlord, certainly dead. Everything one loved and hated gone in the same blast. Big bang. Expanding universe. No boundaries but limited. No name. Not Tomi or Steven.

Jan's groans became more regular, closer together. Finally her eyes opened, glazed with the pain of a contraction. Michael ran into the hall and called Teri, then crept up next to Jan to hold her hand on the bed. The sheets were soaked with her sweat. She lay in a small puddle of thick blood, arching her neck to stare at Michael. "The baby, Michael, it's coming."

"Yes." Michael was surprised to hear his own voice, calm and confident. "You're okay. Just concentrate. You'll be fine."

Jan's eyes became more glassy with the next contraction. Michael looked desperately at the door for Teri to come. "Oh, God," Jan shouted, but as the pain subsided Jan breathed deeply. "Michael. This baby is the promised one."

Michael wondered if she was delirious. He wanted to check her blood pressure, her pulse. He desperately wished he had some

equipment, even just a stethoscope, somethi[ng]
something that would prove she was okay, th[

Jan knew he didn't believe her. "Michae[l
your heart. This baby is the one who is to com[
Michael...Oh, God..." A contraction cut off h[er
loudly and grabbed at his sleeve, holding ont[
teeth. Again the pain subsided. She glared at [
skepticism. "You wait and see. Camille told [
God so loved the world..." Another contracti[on
fell into a consciousness where he could not [
certain.

Teri came in with Bea. Michael moved [
pulled back the sheets. Teri ran for some to[
dilation. The contractions came quickly, with [
them. Jan hardly noticed; she twitched wild[
Teri hurried back into the living room to star[
boiling water to sterilize Bea's equipment.

"Michael, hold her!" Bea shouted at him [
he hurried to his wife's side. Jan crouched [
pushing again and again. An hour passed wit[
peace. The women bustled back and forth, [
birthing tools and getting more water.

During that hour the sky began chan[
black gave way to indigo. Messages had bee[
the mountain and the house starting filling w[
with blank faces. Neighbors. No words for [

Teri returned to the bedroom with mor[
on a wet rag. "What are these people doing h[
Teri shrugged. "Get rid of them," Bea grow[

Helplessly Michael wandered into the [
stood in the doorways. The living room was [
Someone put out a hand to stroke Michael'[
arrived, dirty and tattered. No one questio[
break the hush of the waiting.

At the sight of Camille, confusion ove[
got to go," he pleaded with the group. No [
movement at all, and he wondered if the w[

With another push Jan delivered the afterbirth and, placing the placenta in a bowl, Teri and Bea moved away to the far side of the room. Bea mumbled. "It may live. Did you see the eyes? Do you think his brain is swollen? I can't imagine that is the bone; how would it have gotten through the birth canal? God, how can such a creature stay alive even to be born?"

Teri just shook her head. "His color is good and the heartbeat was strong."

Bea kept speaking under her breath. "Maybe the swelling is water, or what was to be the baby's brain. Hell, maybe it can stay alive, maybe for awhile."

Jan continued stroking the baby. "Our baby. Little one. Look, Michael. He's looking at you." Michael watched Jan. "See, Michael," she whispered. "See, I told you. The one. The promised one."

Michael nodded slightly. The crooked arm. The swollen eyes. Twisted ears. He'd never seen such a thing, never imagined such a child was possible, not even in dreams, his new baby.

Bea came up next to Jan to check her pulse and slip another towel under Jan's hips. She kept her eyes averted until Jan touched her hand. Then their eyes met, hers tired, Jan's calm. Jan whispered to her, "It's okay, Bea. Really, it's fine. What did you expect?"

Bea gasped and stared at Jan. Bea had seen the expression on Jan's face somewhere before. Then she realized; Jan had something of the baby's own unearthly expression.

People were crowding into the bedroom doorway and hall as the sun filled the sky with brilliant morning light. Camille squeezed a neighbor's hand, exchanging a knowing glance. The vigil was kept. Jan held the child close, touching his body, and noticing nothing but the newborn's tiny facial expressions. Now her own body was limp and she did not try to speak. Bea and Teri moved around her. Michael helped Jan put the baby to her breast.

Down by the beach Koken stepped back from the tower. He'd worked hard all day and all night he'd continued mounting the lamp and connecting wires by the light of a flashlight and hurricane lamp. So close to being finished, he was unable to stop working. Feeling the exhilaration in his muscles, he knew the switch could be turned on now. The gasoline line was hooked up to the generator and the gas tank was filled. He flipped the switch and listened to the hum. Then he turned on the monitor, hearing the SOS signal clearly as the large lamp threw its beam across the still water. Back and forth the light passed, bright enough so it could have been seen several miles across the ocean. The sun was rising and its light overtook the lamp's light.

December 26

Jan Ito's baby was born, the first baby conceived and born in the new times. Jan cares for it as any mother might, seemingly oblivious to its deformities yet careful to avoid any pressure against its head, and attending to its peculiar needs. Teruko has stayed in attendance, the two women rocking the baby hour after hour. The baby never cries. The women play the game endlessly and I can no longer follow its rhythm: "Elephants in a zoo—wine—piano concerts—bread."

The epidemic has run its course, and recently three more women have reported pregnancies. We will have to wait and see if theirs will be as handicapped as the Ito's child. Nothing is normal in that baby's physiology, and still, it breathes.

As it turns out, the island is dotted with several "hot spots", radioactive areas where contaminated soil and water collected. Exposure to these spots may have been the cause of many of the deaths in recent months. We should have expected that. Now we wander over the island in fear of what we cannot see. This small plot of ground in the ocean, still harboring a few human lives, is not a safe home. We try to map out the dangers, but it is not always possible. A few families will attempt to make a life on the very small island of Pua.

I have begun to suspect that the mainland, perhaps all of the Northern Hemisphere, has had its life extinguished. I look to South America, perhaps parts of Asia and Africa, and pray that pockets of life may thrive where the poison did not touch.

I do what I have to. The face of the baby is always before me.

July 10

"He grew up before God like a young plant
whose roots are in parched ground;
he had no beauty, no majesty to draw our eyes,
no grace to make us delight in him;
his form, disfigured, lost all the likeness of a man,
his beauty changed beyond human semblance...

He was pierced for our transgressions,
tortured for our iniquities;
the chastisement he bore is health for us
and by his scourging we are healed."

Isaiah, 53